Praise for Claire Cameron's

The Bear

#1 Bestseller in Canada

Long-listed for the Baileys Women's Prize for Fiction
(Formerly the Orange Prize)

Winner of the Northern Lit Award from the Ontario Library Service

"A gripping survival thriller.... Cameron unspools the adventure in Anna's twitchy voice, heightening the tension as the youngsters battle storms, cold, hunger, and fear.... But this agonizing odyssey of loss and being lost has humor.... The book's anguished yet hopeful ending provides a touching terminus.... This expertly crafted novel could do for camping what *Jaws* did for swimming."   —Richard Eisenberg, *People*

"A can't-put-down adventure.... The struggle to survive and find a way home makes for heart-pounding action, but it's Anna's heroics—and her naive, imaginative perspective—that keep you glued to the page. A tender, terrifying, poignant ride. Hang on."   —Leigh Newman, Oprah.com

"An emotional tour de force. Claire Cameron's *The Bear* offers us an unforgettable child narrator who propels us through a story as unsettling as it is bone-chilling, and as suspenseful as it is moving."   —Megan Abbott, author of *Dare Me*

"*The Bear* is a taut and touching story of how a child's love and denial become survival skills. Claire Cameron takes a fairy-tale situation of children pitted against the wilderness, removes the fairies, and adds a terrifying and ravenous bear. I devoured this wonderful new novel in one day—if I can use the word 'devoured' for a book about a bear."

—Charlotte Rogan, author of the national bestseller
The Lifeboat

"Bold....An interesting portrayal of how young minds cope with abandonment, the loss of authority and guidance, survival, and grief....Cameron manages on the whole to capture a childish view of the world with authenticity and charm."

—Flemmich Webb, *The Independent* (UK)

"A page-turner....*The Bear* creates suspense out of the gap between what Anna knows and what the reader suspects....The story is laced with humor and moments of joy and triumph as well as fear and sorrow....Anna is such a compelling character....So gripping that it is hard to put the novel down."

—Margaret Quamme, *Columbus Dispatch*

"Few writers are brave enough to write from the perspective of a small child....With *The Bear,* Canadian writer Claire Cameron does just that: using a real-life bear attack in an Ontario provincial park as the basis for a story of survival. It's a thrilling premise....Anna's memories provide much-needed backstory, allowing Cameron to show a fully formed family and make sure Anna's parents are multidimensional."   —Noah Cruickshank, *The Onion's* A.V. Club

"With remarkable bravery for so pint-size a narrator, Anna explains all that she sees, feels, and lacks as she navigates her and her brother's survival alone in the woods. Anna's perspective and innocence despite the horror of her reality is what will endear the reader."　　　　　　　—Claire Luchette, Bustle.com

"Thrilling and harrowing.... I couldn't put this book down. And I must say that the ending was so right, I caught myself holding my breath. A remarkable novel."

　　　　　　　—Anthony De Sa, author of *Kicking the Sky*

"A vividly portrayed wilderness ordeal (poison ivy, hunger, rain, isolation) juxtaposed with glimpses of the inner resources young Anna draws upon (imagination, family, memory, hope), all seen through the eyes of a child who can express, if not entirely understand, her own resentment and protectiveness of her brother, her love and longing for her parents, her fear and empathy for the predator, and her determination to persevere.... Uplifting."

　　　　　　　—*Publishers Weekly*

"Harrowing suspense. *The Bear* is a survival thriller that is told from a child's-eye view, which not only is convincing but doubles the tension. A heartbreaking, white-knuckle read."

　　　　　　　—Andrew Pyper, author of *The Demonologist*

"A straightforward adventure with a narration that nicely captures an ordinary child's way of thinking—and of blocking out unwelcome knowledge.... Darkly funny.... Harrowing but ultimately hopeful."　　　　　　　—*Kirkus Reviews*

"*The Bear* faultlessly captures the wonder, bewilderment, fear, and self-centeredness of five-year-old Anna, and beautifully balances the darkness of her tale with a hopeful, sensitively told backstory and moments when she grasps her situation with just enough clarity to shoulder her burden."

—Cathy Marie Buchanan, author of *The Painted Girls*

"A taut and engrossing look at an essential web of connected questions: how children think, how families work, how we relate to nature at its most brutal, and how we process grief and trauma.... Cameron proves masterly in the creation of a child's fractured worldview, as familiar as it is unexpected, as observant as it is naive. The result is ideal hibernation reading...the sort of book you'll easily read in one sitting but immediately regret having rushed through. Fortunately, Cameron's resonant plot and Anna's unforgettable voice add up to a novel destined to stay with you long after you've chewed through it."

—Jared Bland, *Globe and Mail*

"Claire Cameron has written a chilling, beautiful, voice-driven novel, one that will turn your blood cold, make you laugh, and remind you of all the ways you are human. Most important she honors the complexity of our relationship with nature, the ways we are humbled by it and tethered to it. A vivid, potent, and unforgettable novel."

—Megan Mayhew Bergman, author of *Birds of a Lesser Paradise*

"A hauntingly beautiful novel about the unspoken bond between mothers and children."

—Miriam Toews, author of *All My Puny Sorrows*

"Heartbreaking, brave, and even funny.... Anna's dreams and fantasies blend into her impressions of reality in a way that seems completely genuine and age-appropriate. Of course, the distance between Anna's circumstances and her understanding of them offers rich potential for narrative irony, which in Cameron's story is most frequently utilized to evoke pathos but is also employed to provide humor.... Readers' hearts will ache as they realize how little Anna understands and how much sadness she has yet to absorb. Equally affecting, however, is the realization of how much Anna *does* know—about courage, survival, and, most of all, love." —Norah Piehl, Bookreporter.com

"*The Bear* is a gut-wrenching trip through the Canadian wilderness with a five-year-old as your guide, a roller coaster of emotions as you hope and pray Anna and her two-year-old brother, Alex, make it to safety before they succumb to the perils of wilderness, including the lack of food and a man-hungry bear. Whew.... Heart-wrenching.... Very engaging. Bittersweet and lovely. If you liked the childlike voice of *Room,* you'll be captivated here." —Kelly Konrad, *ChicagoNow*

The Bear

ALSO BY CLAIRE CAMERON

The Line Painter

BEAR
THE

A NOVEL

CLAIRE CAMERON

BACK BAY BOOKS
LITTLE, BROWN AND COMPANY
NEW YORK   BOSTON   LONDON

Copyright © 2014 by Line Painter Productions
Reading group guide © 2015 by Line Painter Productions and Little, Brown and Company

Back Bay Books / Little, Brown and Company
Hachette Book Group
1290 Avenue of the Americas, New York, NY 10104
littlebrown.com

Originally published in hardcover by Little, Brown and Company, February 2014
First Back Bay paperback edition, February 2015

Back Bay Books is an imprint of Little, Brown and Company. The Back Bay Books name and logo are trademarks of Hachette Book Group, Inc.

The publisher is not responsible for websites (or their content) that are not owned by the publisher.

The Hachette Speakers Bureau provides a wide range of authors for speaking events. To find out more, go to hachettespeakersbureau.com or call (866) 376-6591.

Library of Congress Cataloging-in-Publication Data
Cameron, Claire.
  The bear : a novel / Claire Cameron.—First Edition.
    pages cm
  ISBN 978-0-316-23012-4 (hc) / 978-0-316-23009-4 (pb)
  1. Bear attacks—Algonquin Provincial Park (Ont.)—Fiction.
2. Parents—Death—Fiction. 3. Camping—Algonquin Provincial Park
(Ont.)—Fiction. 4. Brothers and sisters—Fiction. 5. Survival—Algonquin
Provincial Park (Ont.)—Fiction. 6. Algonquin Provincial Park (Ont.)—Fiction.
7. Psychological fiction. I. Title.
  PR9199.4.C3453B43 2014
    813'.6—dc23   2013038910

10 9 8 7 6 5 4 3 2 1

RRD-C

Printed in the United States of America

To Dave, Ben, Max, Keith

"There is a land of the living and a land of the dead and the bridge is love, the only survival, the only meaning."

—*The Bridge of San Luis Rey,*
Thornton Wilder

Contents

Author's Note

In October of 1991, Raymond Jakubauskas and Carola Frehe pitched their tent on Bates Island on Lake Opeongo in Algonquin Park, nearly three thousand square miles of wilderness situated two hundred miles northeast of Toronto. The couple had planned to camp for a three-day weekend. When they failed to return on Monday, friends contacted the police. The partially eaten remains of Jakubauskas and Frehe were found on Wednesday. A large male black bear was standing guard over the prey.

Both victims had died as a result of a broken neck from a blow to the head. To the extent that the events can be reconstructed, it appears that the couple arrived on the island, set up camp, and was preparing a meal when the attack occurred. Frehe was most likely the first to be assaulted. It seems that Jakubauskas attempted to fight off the bear with an oar, since a broken oar was discovered at the campsite and the bear later found to be responsible had long bruises on its body.

In an article about the incident in the book *The Best of the Raven,* park naturalist Dan Strickland remembers the phone calls received after the attack. Many callers wanted to understand why the attack occurred. Strickland says that the bear had no signs of disease or other conditions that might drive it to attack humans. Menstruation, which is often thought to be a cause for bear interest in humans, did not play a role. The other question callers had was about the bear's attraction to food. Although the couple had been cooking at the time of the attack, an untouched tray of ground beef was found at the campsite five days later. The couple's cooking was not the main attraction.

Why did this attack happen? In very rare instances, a black bear will prey on humans—and in these cases, the predator is usually a wild bear rather than a "garbage" bear, which scavenges around campsites and is familiar with humans. Jakubauskas and Frehe did not make mistakes in setting up their camp or do anything foolish once there. Since the bear was a large animal, weighing 308 pounds, it is difficult to say that they could have put up a better fight.

There is no clear reason for what happened other than that a hungry bear decided to take a chance on a new source of food. What is most frightening about this explanation is the idea that there is no blame to place on either the people or the bear. Identifying fault can comfort us because it provides a way to isolate the circumstances of an incident from our own situation, ensuring that what happened to these people will not happen to us. But in this case there is no apparent rationale for the attack other than predation. The couple happened to be in the wrong place at the wrong time.

In the summer of 1991 and 1992, I worked as a counselor at a summer camp in Algonquin Park, leading groups of teenagers on canoe trips that ranged from seven to fourteen days in duration. After the attack, I heard many stories and theories about what had happened on Bates Island—whispers around a campfire at night, all of us searching for the consolation of control, the comfort of story.

The Bear is based on my memories of and research into this bear attack. I added the kids.

—*C.C.*

Part I

Bates Island, Lake Opeongo,
Algonquin Park, 1991

1.

I can hear the air going in and out of my brother's nose. I am awake. He is two years old and almost three and he bugs me lots of times because I am five years old and soon I will be six but it is warm sleeping next to him. I call him Stick. He always falls asleep before me and I listen to the air of his nose. I can hear my parents' voices. They are farther away than I can reach and whispering because they think I can't hear. I let out a squeak to let Momma know I am awake and she says "We're right here" from too far away. I squeak again and the tent zipper undoes and I can see the sky in the crack. Her cool hand brushes my hair back and her fingers touch my cheek. "Shh, Anna," she says and the sky zips away again. When I am inside a tent the outside is far away.

The tent is blue and sniffs like dust. My parents have a fire because it is the end of summer and they are cooking something too and not sharing with me. Bacon. I love bacon. My tummy rumbles and I want bacon but it will make Daddy mad. I sniff Gwen teddy bear instead. She is brown and smells like us. I hear the air whistle when it leaves Sticky's nose. I feel nervous and I don't know why. The night will be dark soon. And it might be the meat is making my tummy weird. When we were back at the cottage, Sticky was chewing on bacon and he shoved another in his mouth and another and another. When Momma saw she said "Chew your food" but Stick couldn't chew because his mouth was all full. He started to go red and his eyes got watery and I thought he was crying. I said "Ha-ha Alex's crying" and Momma came and thumped him. A ball of bacon came out of his mouth. Momma got Stick in trouble for not chewing and I looked at the meat. It had spit on it. I felt a barf in my mouth. And I didn't eat that bacon ball but it's making my tummy feel weird.

The air is cold. I roll closer to Stick. His breath goes in my ear and it is warm. A little piece of light from the fire is having a dance on the side of the tent but only a little because it is not dark yet. There is no music except Stick's nose air and still the light flicks and rolls on the side of the tent. I can't sleep. I tuck Gwen under the covers so she isn't cold and I creep over to the door. The zipper has teeth that grab onto my skin. I go slow so it doesn't bite and I open it just a little bit so my face can be out. The carpet here is made of pine needles. They smell like the yellow bottle I use to help Momma clean the bathtub. There are prickle pine trees all around our camp. These are the ones that forgot the needles on the ground. The moon is going to switch with the sun and the moon will have a tail that shows up on the water. The water is not chop chop chop anymore. It sits quietly in the lake now because it is sleeping. Close to the water, really far away from me, I can see two shadows. I can hear from the whispers that it's Momma and Daddy and they are laughing. Momma leans forward and I see a ponytail like a horse's hanging down. Her face is smiling and I can see her teeth in a nice way. The only other thing I can see is Coleman.

Coleman is green like grass and he is so heavy I can't lift him up. We bring him on canoe trips to carry our food and keep it cold. And we use him so that bears can't rob the food from us. Bears like our food if we let them and we don't want to do that. So Coleman holds everything cool inside his body and has a metal tooth in the front that keeps him shut tight. He is really really big and a metal box. Stick and I can both fit inside him like when we play hide and seek at home. We can stay so quiet and hide in Coleman from Daddy and try to stop laughing with my hand on Stick's mouth. When Coleman sits in the canoe he can't fit across sideways and so Daddy needs to put him pointing to the front. Only Daddy can lift him up. When Coleman has to pee he has a little button at the side where I can push and his pee comes out and when I see it sometimes I pee too. Coleman is why we camped on the island because he is so heavy and big. The water was chop chop chop because the wind was whistling in my ears and Coleman makes the canoe go tippy. If we went down the path to the next lake where we were supposed to camp then Daddy would have to carry Coleman and the canoe but Momma wanted to be here at the island to see the tail of the moon. Once I tried to pick Coleman up and I can't.

I whisper hello to Coleman and Daddy's head turns away from the fire: "Back in the tent, Anna."

I stay still to make me dream.

"Did you hear me?"

I am awake.

"Last time, okay?"

"Yes, Daddy."

"Sleep tight."

I poke my head inside and Gwen missed me. She looks lonely and I tell her with my eyes that I am coming. I carefully take the zipper in my fingers. They feel furry in the tips and too tired to pull. Zipper will bite if I don't watch out. I pull again and the zipper tries to get me between my thumb and pointy finger, the soft part that looks like it could be on a frog. I sit back and pull my hand away. The zipper must be hungry and so I will stay away. I grab Gwen and sniff and tuck her back into the sleeping bag.

I lie on my back and snuggle and the fire is dancing more on the side of the tent because it is a little more blue and gray outside. I watch it and my eyes start to shut but I don't want them to. Maybe if Stick is asleep then Momma will pluck me out of bed and feed me bacon. I want to ask out loud but my teeth are too fuzzy. My head is heavy like a rock. My eyes shut again and I peel them open. I hear a sniff. It might have been from Sticky's nose but it sounded bigger than that. Stick's nose must be growing and in the middle of the night it will hog all the air. Something moves on the side of the tent. I see some fluff beside the dancing fire and I think the fluff is Stick's hair. He has escaped. It might be his little white head sneaking out for bacon. A few of his fluffy hairs are sticking up as a shadow just outside the tent. His nose whistles beside me so I know it's not, but the hair stands up and I think it looks thicker. The hair stands there shaking like my fingers when I am hungry. I watch it and it moves forward only a very little, as slow as a snail. It would be a hairy snail and much bigger and that means it probably isn't a snail anymore. And the bacon smells and my eyes fall down and now I can open them only a crack. I see the hair move and I think as my eye shuts how did Stick stay sleeping and sneak out of the tent for bacon at the same time?

2.

I hear Momma yelling and I keep my eyes closed. Dreams aren't real. I know that because my momma doesn't yell. She has a soft voice that looks like a lily that tastes like sugar cookies at Christmas when you don't put the sprinkles on. We made cookies and I was allowed to use the shiny stamp to make an angel. The wings broke off in the oven and then we tried again and we got perfect angels with wings. Stick wanted to eat his before Momma put the sprinkles on. He cried because he couldn't wait for sprinkles and thought we were just taking the cookie from him. Momma gave him the cookie and he ate it and I put icing on mine. Red and green icing and sprinkles even though they blinked like the sun when I held them up. I got done and wanted to save my cookie to show Daddy and put it on a plate. Stick started to cry. He wanted my cookie. Momma said no. Stick cried more. Stick loves cookies.

Momma doesn't yell about cookies and she doesn't yell when

I spill my glue on the carpet even though the glue was brand new and it was all gone. She says she only will yell if I am about to get hit by a bus. She says maybe sometimes people yell because things are hard but if you go past the things that are hard you can be very very strong. And now she is yelling. I open my eyes to see if a bus is coming. I will jump out of the way like a superhero, maybe one with a cape but maybe not. All I see is blue and I am lying on my side so it is hard to jump. The whole world looks blue and flappy. I give Gwen a hug and look at the flapping. It's the tent in my face. Flap flap flap—it snaps and growls like a dragon. I better close my eyes so it isn't so scary.

I think of my house in Toronto because I wish I am there. I like the woods too. The pine needles taste like spicy gum and I climb on rocks. I can swim like a dog when I kick hard. And I like coming out into the park near our cottage in a canoe with marshmallows and graham crackers and chocolate that we smoosh together and Stick gets it stuck in his hair and hands. He is Stick because he always has sticky hands. He used to have them more like every time he touched me on the arm his hand would stick on me. And he also plays with sticks all the time. He chops me with them and he pretends that they are cars or trucks or guys. I said one day that he was a sticky stick and Momma and Daddy really laughed because there is one word and he is both of them. That is how he got the name Stick and Daddy lifts his shoulders and says it just stuck.

Right now I like our house in Toronto more and it is brick and tall and skinny. My friend Jessica says hers is bigger. The kitchen is almost in the backyard where there is a tree that is the same age as me. We are growing thicker every year except it has more leaves and is way taller now. I want to catch up. There is a big long counter that I sit at to make cookies and eat cereal. Also Popsicles because in the backyard is where you go so they won't drip. Sometimes I used to let my tongue melt it a little and let it drip into my tree. Now I don't do that because the magic drip made the tree grow so fast that it is way bigger than me even though we are the same age. That's why I like my kitchen but my favorite place in my house is my room. It has my puzzles and Lego and a carpet that tickles my feet. I go under the sheets with Gwen. We hide in bed when it is rainy outside the door or when I feel scared. I call and Daddy comes in to snuggle with me. He never talks. He gets into bed with mussy hair and wraps his arms around me. In the morning I wake up and he is gone.

When you have a dream and it feels real it means you might pee the bed. That's what Momma says. If I am having a bad dream she says I should get up and pee. The bathroom light is always on. But I remember the tent. That is what is blue and very flappy. Flap flap flap. Maybe I am dreaming that too. The most important thing that Momma says I have to remember is not to dream I am going pee before I get to the toilet. It's not my fault but I have to remember. If I don't remember and I dream that I am peeing then I really pee but not in the toilet. Then I wet the bed and the sheet that makes a crunchy sound like cereal needs to be hung in the backyard on a string so I can hide behind it like the curtain for a play. Go to the toilet. There is no toilet when we are camping. I don't need to pee.

And I don't like the flap flap flap. I turn over and hug Gwen and snuggle into Stick and hope the sounds will go away. Momma screams like a monster is tackling her. That's why I know it's a dream so I should keep my eyes shut tight. It is dark behind my eyes. Momma never yells. Mostly not ever. Except sometimes.

3.

Even though my eyes are shut tight I can hear the rip of the zipper. I turn to look and see a crack of sky and it is really dark blue now and Daddy's head is blocking most of it. He looks mad and I am in trouble. He is shouting and all I see is teeth. They are not very white teeth and big. He has pointy fangs and at the back he has even bigger teeth that are wide and look like they could be in a dinosaur's head. Inside the middle of most of them is a piece of gold. That is where he keeps all our golden treasure so that it will be safe. If it is inside his mouth then no robber can sneak away with it. Or if a robber tries to take it in the night then he will also have to try to take Daddy's teeth. That will wake Daddy up and he will chase the robber away. I duck down. Daddy scoops me up.

Daddy is hugging me but it's not a snuggle. It is hard and squeezy and my breath shoots out of my body. The sky shakes. I see a long arm that is like a claw but big and it is a tree branch with needles. Daddy is running and the running is shaking me. The yelling won't stop. I see Gwen's head jumping up and down. She is in my arm and she will let go if I don't hang on so I pull her tighter and try to sniff but her head is wiggling too much. Daddy jerks me back and I see things scatter all over the ground and I think that Daddy is making a mess.

Daddy moves away fast and I feel the ground go in my back. It is pointy and makes my breath go away. A pine needle pricks in the crack between my pj top and bottom. My pj pants are always falling down. I have to use my hand to pull them up at the back and sometimes when I am running it happens. Once a boy laughed and pointed because he said he saw my bum. He didn't see my bum. Not the round part. Just the tippy top of the crack that peeks out from my pants. Momma says it's my other-end smile. I like pants that stay on.

I want to reach to get my pants up but Daddy grabs my ribs again. He throws me like he does into the water at the lake but there is not water. I hit my head. I scream and it hurts and Daddy is so mad he is yelling. Except he made the mess not me. Or Stick might have sneaked out and made the mess but Daddy is still yelling. He pushes me and I wonder if he is going to throw me into the lake. He does this sometimes but we aren't supposed to play rough in the water. We have to be laughing and everyone needs to be happy if Daddy is going to let me stand on his shoulders and jump or if he is going to throw me in. When I do jump I am not scared. I plug my nose and go in and the noise stops. It is quiet under the water. There are bubbles that I see and no sharks. They don't live in our lake. Only little fish that nibble at my toes if I stand really still and even that doesn't hurt. When it is quiet and I see the bubbles I know it is time to go up and I let go of my nose. I kick my legs and come back up and find Daddy's arm to hold me up. The noises push back in my ears.

This time Daddy throws me and I don't go in the water. There is something hard in my back and Daddy pushes at my stomach. It is not a game. We aren't supposed to push so I tell him to stop and scream because he is screaming so many things that I don't think he can hear me. He pushes again even though it is not allowed and it hurts my stomach this time so I curl into a ball around Gwen. He shoves me on the back and I feel the air rush around me. I hear a thump. Click.

I am in the black. And I am mad at Daddy. He is shouting and pushing and both those things are naughty and I wonder if he is getting in trouble from Momma. When Momma gets mad she doesn't yell. She looks at me and she lets the sad drip up from her heart through her veins and into her eyes. Her eyes send the sad into my eyes and then it drips back down into my heart and makes it feel like a ball. But not a ball that bounces up high—one that is squishy because it needs Daddy to put in air. I won't ask Daddy to pump my heart because I am so mad. I can't see him anymore. It is so so dark. I don't know if my eyes are open or shut. I think they are shut and I put my finger to see. I can feel my eyelid. After I know then I open my eyes and it looks exactly the same. My eye feels sad.

Momma leaves a night-light on when it is too dark. I stick my hand out. All I feel is a smooth wall. I know how it feels and it is Coleman.

The air goes whoosh and the light comes back from the sky. I see Daddy's face. His eyes look like they are in a cartoon when a guy gets hit. Then I see Stick is in the air above me and he is coming down. His legs are curled up and his face looks like when he got stung by the bee in our backyard. He was in his high chair when he was a baby and the bee wanted his food. It ran into his forehead but the bee took the stinger away. Stick didn't need a needle but his face went all red and it scrunched up into the middle. So now he maybe got stung by a bee and Daddy pushes him in beside me and I say "Hey" because there is not room and Stick's feet are touching me. I try to push him away and Daddy gets even madder. He has snaky veins on the side of his neck under his skin and he yells so loud I cover my ears and hunch my shoulders up. I am bad. Very bad. Again. I didn't wet the bed and I can't remember what I did to get him so mad but I never really do.

"Stay in there," he yells and sounds sick. "Don't get out."

Maybe Stick was bad.

Daddy squishes us down and it gets dark again. I feel the air whoosh and a thump and a click. Coleman shuts his mouth. The air from Stick's nose goes in and I almost can't breathe. And then it opens a crack and I feel the cool air again and take a breath. I see Daddy's fingers and a rock. The fingers put the rock at the side of Coleman's mouth where he has no teeth and it sticks there and Coleman's mouth closes down. There is a click from the metal tooth at the front of Coleman and Daddy is yelling at me not to touch the rock and that it is my problem rock. Coleman can't shut his mouth all the way because the rock is there at the side. Daddy moves away and now he is yelling at Momma. She won't like it. I stick my ear to the crack of Coleman's mouth and I hear Daddy yelling.

"The paddle...oh, my God."

He says God, not Jesus.

We are inside Coleman. Stick's toes stick into my leg and I don't like it. There is not enough room for both of us. When we share a bed, Momma draws a line down the middle and no one's toes are allowed over the line. I say there is a line and try to draw it with my chopper hand down the middle. I can't draw the line without Stick's bum leaking over. I kick him to get him on his side of the line and he cries and there is yelling and Momma is yelling back and Daddy is roaring and sounds like a lion with a big mane that shakes. I don't like this Daddy that is shouting so much. I want the other Daddy back but he keeps yelling even though Momma isn't. Momma doesn't yell so I feel better. I like her quiet because that's what she is.

I push Stick with my feet for more room. It is too squishy in Coleman for us. Now his bum is in my face and I don't want it there. His nose breath is hot on me and I don't want it there either. I put my head up to put my nose by the crack in Coleman's mouth. I can see the rock is stuck between Coleman's mouth like a tooth on the side. I am not allowed to touch the rock. I put my nose up to the air so that Stick doesn't hog all mine. I can hear huffing and it might be the new Daddy. There is a huff and a growl and I hear Daddy talking like he is sad. He keeps talking and his voice is quieter so maybe my daddy is coming back and there is a snarl and a growl and I don't know what it is. I try to push my head up but my forehead is tall. It stands up from my eyes until my hair so I can't make my eyes get right in Coleman's mouth to see through his lips. I am glad that Coleman isn't a whale with a big tongue that would suck me back. Whales don't have teeth so we could get sucked in on a waterfall that was really just how the whale eats. The whale doesn't want to eat us but he doesn't know we are there because he has no ears on his head and won't hear even if Stick cries. A whale doesn't eat people he eats trees.

Stick and I have to wait for trees to flow into the whale's mouth. We sit in the middle. If a tree comes in and we catch it and maybe another then I could use a rope to tie the trees together to make a boat to float on top of. We could float out of the mouth when the whale was sleeping one day but then we would float back in by accident. But I can't do any of my plan because Stick pulls my hair and I punch him back and I see that it is only Coleman's mouth that we are in but I still feel shakes. There is no whale. Stick can't swim.

I can hear things outside Coleman. My ear is close to his mouth so I can hear more than the inside sounds of Stick's nose and whining. Outside I hear a growl and a nose breath that isn't Stick's. It's from a longer nose like Snoopy's. He is a dog that lives next door and usually he is behind the fence and he barks at Stick and me when we play with a ball. At first when I met him I got scared because Snoopy is big. His name was wrong because he didn't look like he does in the TV. He is black and tall and inside his mouth there is black. He stared at me like I would be a good dinner or my arm is a chew toy. My momma said hello to Snoopy after a while and then we were friends. Now Snoopy gets in our yard and takes my ball but I share. Only with Snoopy not with Stick. Snoopy will run after my ball and bring it back again and again and again. He is the only person who will play ball with me for a long enough time because Momma only throws twice or one more time and then that's all the times and I'm alone and that isn't so good. And Stick's hands are too fat to catch so Snoopy is the best. I can hear Snoopy outside of Coleman and it's not Toronto but Snoopy came to visit near the cottage and maybe doesn't like it because he growls. Mrs. Buchanan must miss Snoopy or maybe she came to see me too. Snoopy's voice is low and he makes a woof woof woof. And I hear Daddy talking and I wonder why he has so much to say to Snoopy when usually he does not. Except for if Snoopy makes a poo and leaves it in our yard.

4.

Stick cries so much. I call Daddy and Momma and my throat feels like the deck at the cottage that gives me splinters in my foot. No one is coming. I don't like splinters and I don't want one in my throat. This is bad. This must be how we do time-out when we are camping. It's not like a normal time-out in Toronto or when I am at the cottage. I don't sit on a step or on the porch. Here I sit inside Coleman. But I haven't talked and I stayed still and I was quiet for as long as the time-out and still Daddy won't let me out. I try to stick my eyes out Coleman's mouth but my forehead is still too tall. I see stars and the wind is not breathing. I call Daddy and Momma again and no one. I listen and I can hear other breath, not wind or Stick's nose. The noises are Snoopy breathing. Mrs. Buchanan has given Snoopy a bone. I am not allowed to but Mrs. Buchanan lets me hold the bone out and Snoopy takes it. He does it gentle with his lips back so that I can see his teeth aren't going to bite me and he keeps them far away from my hand. When he is done with the bone for his dinner he gives me a wet kiss on the cheek and I smile.

Snoopy is eating the bone and I can hear the snap snap snap of his jaws on the bone. His nose is snuffling because he is a pig when he eats and doesn't stop to breathe. I am supposed to stop to breathe even when I am so so hungry. Snoopy doesn't stop because he is a dog. His teeth go scrape on the bone and I hear it pop. I think Snoopy has broken the bone and he's not supposed to do that. It can get stuck in the roof of his mouth and he has to go to the dog hospital. It happened once but I wasn't there. Mrs. Buchanan told me. Snoopy cried at the vet and got a needle to make him sleeping so they could get the bone out. And the sounds outside crack crack snap and I know that Snoopy has broken the bone but Mrs. Buchanan is not stopping him. Maybe she is sleeping because it is nighttime for her.

"Snoop," I call out of Coleman's mouth.

He doesn't listen. He keeps eating.

"Hey, Snoop!"

I say it louder. Behind me I feel Stick twisting. He puts a knee in my back but he is quiet and maybe having a snooze. I don't want to wake him up because he stopped whining after so long.

"Snooooopeeee," I whisper.

The chewing stops and I hear Snoopy sniffing.

The sniffing gets louder. Snoopy is coming to see me. I stick my fingers out to say hello because I have one hand that isn't holding Gwen. There is a bad smell. I pull my fingers in to plug my nose up because my nostrils don't like the smell. Snoopy needs a bath. It smells like the rotting leaves under the cottage and when there were fish guts in the boat. Yuck. Snoopy comes and I see his big nose sniffing in the crack but his smell is wrong and it gives me the shakes and I don't know why except the smell of fish. I don't like fish to eat. The crack goes dark and there is hair coming in the crack. It is not like Snoopy's. It is more prickly hair and fills up the crack and turns out the lights and I can't see. And Stick starts to cry because it is dark and we get jerked. Stick pushes into me and I grab Gwen and Coleman shakes and it is still dark and I call Daddy. We shake harder and I hear huff and it stinks. I cover my mouth because I don't want to breathe in the smell and Stick is crying and then I am too and we shake more and we flip. I roll back and my head goes clunk on Coleman. There is growling and a sound like Momma is making lunch and using the top of Coleman to cut apples with a knife. But it is not Momma because her hair is yellow and she always gives me a piece of apple first. It is louder and more like there are ten Mommas cutting apples but that is too many and they wouldn't fit. And it is dark flashing on and off and I can see Stick on his side crying and I need Daddy because it isn't Snoopy and I am not supposed to talk to strange dogs because we don't know them. I'm on my back and Stick gets shoved into me but I don't mind and I grab his arm and pull him and Gwen in and we cry and scrape scrape scrape. I see the fur and hear too much breath and squeeze Stick and Gwen and my eyes shut tight and we cry.

My tears are gone when the scraping stops. Coleman stays on his back with the rock in his mouth. The black dog is not scratching Coleman. He goes back to his sniffing and huffing and then he starts cracking his bone. Stick and I are huddled in tight. Stick's head is heavy like a bowling ball and it makes my arm go fuzzed and he snuggles in. It is so dark outside Coleman and no Daddy or Mommy and after a while I watch the lids of my eyes close down like jaws.

5.

I open my eyes and it is light outside Coleman now and I can see Stick's crying face all red and squishy. He cries for Momma. I tell him to shush. He keeps crying. His belly is squishy too. It looks like a ball and is round like his cheeks. His face is like a bad tomato because he is crying so much. It is wet and he has snots all over his nose. It is very noisy inside Coleman because of Sticky and I'd like to get out.

I call Daddy and Momma and no one comes. I try to have a peek outside. I can see a line of sky that is blue. The trees reach out and they don't look like claws anymore. I put my hands over my ears because it is so loud from Stick crying and I squint my eyes too. It is still loud but I can see darker lines down my eyes. I open them and the lines are gone. I shut them and they come back. The lines are attached to my eyes. I touch and they are my eyelashes. I thought they were skinnier but they look furry. In the mirror there are a lot of eyelashes but with my squinty eyes there are gaps in between. I can still see out. The tree branches look furry not like claws. Like the needles are the eyelashes of a tree. And they are furry in the same way. When I squint. It is too loud and my hands on my ears barely block all the noise.

After a while Stick's crying stops and I take my hands off. Stick is only breathing through his spit. He is curled up on his side of Coleman and just staring at the blank wall. It is hard to lift my head so I put it back down and listen. I hear nothing except then I do. I hear a sniff.

The sniffing is closer. I think of the black dog I saw through the crack. I don't think Snoopy is here. Snoopy would listen and be nice. Mrs. Buchanan would call Snoopy because she doesn't like him to be very far away. I hear more sniffs and I don't hear Mrs. Buchanan. I think it is the black dog and I feel scared. I was scared of Snoopy too. The black dog might not be bad. I keep my fingers away from the crack because you are not supposed to make your fingers look like carrots.

The sniffing is close and something bumps Coleman. He wiggles and then stops. Sniffing and another bump. The black dog's nose comes to the crack. It is wet so the black dog isn't sick. It is big. It looks shiny like the chair at my grandpa's house. Grandpa loves to sit. He says his "old bones" need a chair and there is a handle that I pull on the side. I am only allowed to pull the handle when Grandpa is ready for his legs to kick up. My grandpa is very nice when I do things his way and so I do. The chair is black and sometimes the cleaning lady rubs a cloth on it so much that I can nearly see my nose. Not my real nose but like a shadow of my nose. Rose. That is the cleaning lady. She smells like lemons and wears an apron that I think should have lemons too. Instead it is pink flowers that are more floaty. Rose came after my grandma died and my grandpa missed her so much he got Rose to do her jobs. When I pull the handle on the chair a small toadstool appears from the bottom of the chair and picks up Grandpa's feet until he is lying down like a bed. Except it isn't a bed. It's a black chair. Shiny and smooth with dimples. Like this nose.

The nose sniffs and I watch the nostrils go in and out. Stick is quiet and I only hear him make a small squeak but I don't want to lift my head because the nose is looking at me. It keeps breathing in my air like it's saying hello like Snoop does. Except it's not hello. It's more like who are you? I don't want to talk and I keep my head flat and I feel Stick is moving like he is trying to get away. There is nowhere to go inside Coleman. Stick is wiggling and I want him to stop. I push to get him over more on his side again. His head comes up near mine and our feet are curled together. The nose keeps sniffing around the edge of Coleman's mouth and I take my hand and put it over Stick's mouth like when we hide from Daddy. Not enough to make Stick mad or tight so he can't breathe but I don't want the black dog to know us. Stick's stomach sucks in like he is going to scream and he changes his eyes to look at me. I say shh and I can feel his lips flap open to yell at me but his eyes blink once and he is quiet. I put my hand on him and we are quiet and we watch the nose sniff sniff sniff.

The rock is still stuck in the side of Coleman's mouth. The front of Coleman has the metal tooth that Daddy pushed in to make us stay. The nose finds Coleman's metal tooth and pushes on it. The nose lifts up and a big tongue jumps out. I see a black lip and a tooth that is very white and long. The fur is a little bit wet and there is pink juice on it. I once had a juice box with tomato juice at a party. That was sneaky. Usually it would be apple or orange or fruit juice and this was tomato and I did not like it at all. I spat it out and Daddy said it was a mess. But he wanted me to put the mess in my stomach and that was gross. So I did spit and I said sorry but I didn't think sorry. The black dog has tomato juice on his jaw and some of it paints onto Coleman's white lip. The tongue comes out and licks the juice and keeps licking like Coleman has yummy things stuck on his mouth.

The teeth open and I see the sides scrape along the edge of Coleman and I see little bits of Coleman turn into metal splinters. The black dog is making grunts like it is uncomfy or maybe mad. He is chewing on Coleman like he was a toy and I grab Stick in because I don't like looking at the teeth. There is one that is really long and I start to shake. And the tooth is scraping and ducks under the metal clip and catches there. The tooth is like a hook and Coleman shakes and Stick screams and I think maybe I do too. The fur in the crack snaps back and the tooth isn't a hook even though it tries to be. It comes right back and the mouth pushes and tries to get hooked. It pushes in and fills us with its smell. Bad bad breath. Like rotting stink. The hamburger that Momma forgot in the fridge and only found when it was brown with green fur. Like that except with black fur. Stink. The tooth comes in and looks like a sword and tries to hook. And Stick screams and I can't stand the noise and the stink and my foot is there so I kick.

I hit the tooth and my foot is ouch and I put my foot back in a ball. There is a yelp. A low growl. The stink gets less. We hear sniff sniff sniff and less sniffs. I keep listening and the tooth is not in the crack. The nose isn't either. I hear a scrape and a smacking of lips. The dog is chewing on something. Not Coleman but food that is closer to the lake. Like when I chew on chicken I hear scrape pop smack. The black dog is eating breakfast. It looks like Stick is listening too because his head is up nearer the crack and he turns and looks at me and lifts the front of his shirt up to wipe his nose.

6.

I want to get out of Coleman. We are not allowed to get out of Coleman. Daddy said. I sit still for as long as I can. I can't anymore. Stick is wiggling.

"I get out," he says.

"Daddy said stay," I say in my Daddy grown-up voice.

"Get out."

"Stay."

I turn my shoulder and I want to get out. "Daddy!"

"Get out."

"DADDY."

"Dada."

"DAAAAAAAAAAAAADY!"

Stick and I both yell. And I guess our throats hurt with splinters and after a while we stop. Then there are no sounds. The sky through the crack looks empty of everything. Only blue and one branch with fur. Even the black dog has gone away.

We are quiet, listening. Then a stink comes and I think the black dog has come back. I wave my hand to put the air back outside the crack. It's like the air has stopped coming in. Or Stick has hogged it all. I can't get the air in my nose—it is too thick and full of stink. The air has trouble getting down my throat and I pull up my pj top to try and breathe its air. I put Gwen to my nose to sniff but she is getting clogged too.

"Stick?"

He doesn't answer. He never does.

"Did you poop?"

"Yep."

"DADDY!"

Daddy is gone again.

I kick at Coleman's metal tooth that hangs down the middle of his mouth. He is biting hard and he won't let go. Coleman's metal tooth is pointing to the sky because he is lying on his back when the black dog pushed. I wiggle around to put my mouth up to it and try and bite like the black dog. It is hard to reach and I have to put my knee on Stick's stomach that squishes. Coleman's tooth tastes like metal yuck and I can't even hook my tooth because it is too short. I punch up with my hand and it gives me a red line on my knuckle. Daddy will be mad if I try to get out but the stink is too bad. I punch with my shoulder up and that hurts. Coleman's tooth hooks around a metal thing that looks like his nose on the outside. I put my fingers outside the crack and try to reach the nose and it feels like I am trying to pick it. I hope Coleman doesn't have snot and I laugh. But I can't reach the nose and it hangs on to the metal tooth very tight.

I need to get out of the stink. Gwen will get it on her and she will not smell right. I squint my eyes to make my brain see if

Coleman has any other teeth or noses but I can't think of any. Stick starts to kick me away from his stomach and I tell him to move.

"Stop," he says and pushes me.

"I want to get out of your stink."

"Get out," he says.

"I'm trying."

I push and try to smoosh him right against the side of Coleman to get as far away from his stink as I can. He bunches up his thigh and kicks out with his foot. My chest is already sore and achy and he hits right at my heart. My breath goes whoosh out of my stomach and I hit the top of Coleman and fall to the side. My shoulder hits the back and there is a sharp tooth in it.

"Ow," I scream at Stick.

I punch out and kick him and he screams and I don't care. I kick more because that will make Daddy come. I kick and punch and Sticky is screaming so loud and it stinks and I am crying and the salt drips into my mouth. And my shoulder hurts a lot each time I move so I stop and lift my arm up so I can see. Stick kicks me more but stops when I don't kick back and then just cries. I don't care because I can see there is a red bang on the side of my arm and it is big. I can show that to Daddy when he wants to know who started it. This is Sticky's fault. I look and there is a red mark from the rock in the side of Coleman's mouth. Coleman is on his back and the rock on the side is pushing on my arm.

Every time I wiggle the rock pushes me in the shoulder now. I try to move away from it because I feel really tired but the rock keeps kicking me too. But then I get closer to Stick's poo so I wiggle back again. I don't like the rock and it's Daddy's fault for putting it there. Daddy made a big red hole in my arm. I start to cry but I don't do it out loud. That way Stick won't think he won. I hate the rock and I bang it with my arm. Daddy is bad and Momma should come and snuggle because that's what happens next. Momma yells almost not ever except maybe one time and another and she says she tries so hard not to. I know and so I give her a hug and put my fingers on her cheek where it is soft. Sticky looks asleep because he is so small and he doesn't care. He's almost not a baby anymore but he still is and bugging me. Where is my snuggle from Momma if Daddy didn't leave for a long time just short? That's what I get a snuggle for because I am older than Stick and I know and it is sometimes my job to make Momma feel okay. And she says "I have you, Anna. You are so strong" and we stay in my bed and in the morning she is still snuggled in. Maybe Daddy isn't gone. He will come soon if I just go to sleep. He doesn't hate me. Momma said Daddy will come.

I can't wait so long. I don't know if Daddy is coming this time. This time he isn't coming back. The rock tooth just sits in Coleman's mouth looking stupid and bugging me in the arm. I see that the rock is more inside Coleman than outside so I put my finger under it. I can wiggle the rock. Coleman is biting hard trying to hang on to the rock but his edges are grindy and a white piece of his lip comes off when I push. I wiggle around all the way and that is hard and I put all my fingers under the rock and lift up as hard as I can. One second I am lifting and I give a hard pull and I blink and I open my eyes and there is a loud snap and it is suddenly dark.

It is dark but my eyes are open. Coleman has snapped his jaws shut.

"Nana?" says Stick.

Outside I hear a piece of metal fall and jingle bells on a rock. "Nana?"

He says my name the wrong way round every time and no air and no crack and the stink is so bad my head is swimming because there is no extra room to breathe. I lean over to the side and then I fall down. The crack opens up and I turn to see blue. Stick and I are the eggs and someone whacked our shell against the edge and it got a line that split into more lines and now it broke. Coleman is cracked. We fall out.

Cold air hits my nose and I am so so glad to have more air in my nose. The stink is less already. I try to straighten my legs and they are all fuzzy. It feels like my legs are stumps that got tied to my body. I straighten one out and then the other and I roll out from Coleman into the pine needles that are prickles. It is warm and the sun is hitting the pine needles and they make a nice place. I lie on my back and get the air back in my nose.

I sit up and look over at Stick. He is sitting like a stump beside Coleman. I get worried that we are out of Coleman and we were supposed to stay in. That might make Daddy mad and he will stay away more. It wasn't my fault because Coleman opened his mouth. I wonder if I should get back in. Coleman's metal tooth has dropped off his head and is near a rock on the ground. He won't be able to bite us back in. I feel glad because that's not a good place to be. And I am still feeling glad that Daddy can't be mad but then I see that Stick has a red bang on his cheek from when I punched him and I think that I will get in trouble so maybe Daddy will come back or maybe not. Stick is going to be in trouble for pooping. I don't want to get in trouble. I want Daddy back.

7.

I look around and it's mess mess mess. I didn't make the mess. There are foods all over the ground like they were thrown. It wasn't me. Someone took food and pushed it around the ground. I look down and see an apple and pick it up for a bite. It is good. Someone has already taken a bite and it was probably Stick because he does that and then puts them back in the bowl. Mom picks up the apple that Stick bit and shows it to him and says "Do we have a rat in the kitchen?" This bite is bigger than a rat's or Sticky's but I don't care because I am hungry. I take a bite and it is good. A string of juice runs down my chin. I stick out my tongue and it's apple juice. Yum. I am thirsty. More juice is nice and I wonder if I can stick a straw right into the apple and drink like that. I look around in the mess because I wonder if there is a straw but there isn't because we don't bring straws camping in a canoe.

When we go camping in a canoe sometimes after we go across

a lake there is a path. When Daddy is happy he picks up the canoe and carries it on his head. He shouts from inside and says he is Mr. Canoe Head and does a dance like with tap dancing shoes except he does it with his wet sneakers and his legs sticking out the bottom of the canoe. Stick and I laugh. He starts shouting about Mr. Canoe Head and walking around and it makes his voice big and echo and so that's when it scares Stick. But I am older so I keep laughing. Momma takes the paddles and a bag on her back so that she looks like a turtle. The car isn't here because we have gone in the canoe away from the car for a long time. Stick and I carry our life jackets and I need to take Gwen. We walk on a path behind Mr. Canoe Head until we get to another lake. Mr. Canoe Head puts down the canoe and it becomes a boat again not a head and Daddy becomes him and not two legs. He tells us to wait and that's where Momma and Stick and I play until Daddy comes back. Coleman is important because we only bring the food in Coleman and he knows how to keep animals out of our food so we still have breakfast. And we have more than breakfast because I see there are cookies that Momma made sitting on the ground. They are in a tin that I know because it always has cookies. I pick it up and there are little holes in the tin now. I think Stick tried to get into the tin with a stick. I put my fingers on the edge of the tin because I want a cookie but it is hard to pull. My fingers slip off and I try again. I can't get a cookie and I drop the tin because I am mad and can't see what else fell out of Coleman.

I see a piece of meat on the ground and wrinkle up my nose because I think maybe it stinks. I wish I could smell Gwen instead and she is not in my hand. I look back and see I left her near Coleman all alone so I run and grab her and sniff. She's almost back to normal smell but my eyes go back to the meat. It looks like when I opened the fridge and there was a big long piece that took up a lot of space. It was in a pan and I took a stool to look in and there was dripped blood and I didn't like how it looked. My tummy made a little butterfly inside. Momma saw me looking and told me that I didn't need to worry and that it was a leg. I wanted to know why we keep legs in the fridge and she said it was from a lamb but with no hoof still on and that's why it had blood because lambs have blood inside them. And a lamb eating grass by a farm isn't like this meat or the lamb in our fridge but the grass must go into its body and turn red. I don't like legs or lambs in our fridge and I was glad when I looked the next day and it was gone. And I don't like this meat that the black dog left all on the ground. It doesn't have a hoof on it either and instead it has Daddy's shoe and I don't know why he would have stuck his shoe on the meat but maybe he was trying to help the lamb. There are flies on the meat because it should be in the fridge. There is no fridge and I hear my name.

"Anna."

I look up and I don't know the voice. There isn't anyone else around the camp because I don't know where my parents are.

"Anna."

It's not the wrong way round way like Stick says it. The voice is whispery soft like a ghost and I look up because it must be flying in the branches. I look up and walk a step closer to the place where the campfire is and look around because the ghosts will scare me. The whispery voice says something else and I know there are ghosts because no one who sounds like that knows my name. I look in the canoe that is sitting with its feet in the water over by the fire rocks and there are no ghosts inside. The black log in the fire has a little bit of white coming up from it and it looks like the tail of a ghost.

"Anna."

The ghost whispers from the fire and makes my stomach butterfly jumpy so I bend my knees to sit and hug them and sniff Gwen.

"Here, sweetie. Look."

I turn my head and I see Momma is lying in the plants. There is a flat circle in the camp that is covered by needles and then there is a part with plants that people don't walk around so it's the part where the plants stay. I can't see Momma but I can see the bottom of her foot. Or it's not her foot but it is her shoe. A special shoe that is good for going in a canoe because I should always wear shoes when I am camping. I look down and my feet are standing in the needles and they don't have shoes on them. Little piggy toes sit at the end of my feet and they look pink. Piggy pink. I don't want to put on my shoes I want my mom to put on my shoes. I can't find my shoes and I haven't looked because she will ask but it's too much mess mess mess and my shoes are by the door and there is no door.

My mom has her shoes on because I see one standing up in the plants. The toe points to the sky. These are shoes that you can get wet and they won't stink. They have rubber that helps her not slip on rocks. Even though she did slip on a rock when she was helping Stick to get out of the canoe. He is a heavy little fella and they went tip and the canoe got water in it because the rubber didn't stay on the rock. Stick cried. Momma put him on the side of the water and he got to sit in her lap and cry even though he wasn't really hurt. She hugged him with both her arms around so he was in the warm and soft place and she rocked and said "It's okay; it's okay." Stick cried even though it didn't hurt anymore because he loves sitting on Momma. When he stopped crying she asked him if it was all better and he said "You okay, Momma?" and put his hand on her cheek. He got even more hugs when it should have been my turn. I have to walk there and Momma is not coming here. She would come if it was Stick so that's not fair. The special shoe is sitting up in the plant and it is not far away and I don't like the fire knowing my name.

"That's my momma," I whisper to the ghost.

I don't want the ghost to follow when I walk into the plants and I think of poison ivy. It looks like every other plant and has green leaves that are shiny like all of them everywhere. Momma should be careful. But she doesn't move and then I am beside her and I look and there is blood and I get so scared that my heart jumps in my throat and a frog is in my mouth. She is hiding a little bit in leaves and maybe that is to cover up the blood so I won't see it but I can.

"Anna, it's okay," she whispers and her sound is not hers. "Come here, sweetie."

"Blood."

"It's okay; it's okay." She closes her eyes and it feels like a really long time and I wonder if she fell asleep and then when I'm going to shout to wake her up the eyes pop open. "Come close to me."

The blood is on her neck and in her shirt and it is ripped and she looks like not Momma but a doll. The doll that she had when she was a baby with eyelids that open and shut and a stare that only goes through the wall and not at your eyes. And skin that is dirty and feels too much like apples.

"It's okay. Come so you can hear me."

I bend down and it is still Momma and when I do she is cold but she still smells Momma. I put my cheek close to hers and I feel better because the ghosts won't come when I am close. She doesn't need to talk to them or do the ghost dance or turn back on the lights. Ghosts just know.

So I sit with my cheek touching hers and I am finally safe and I start to feel hot tears because of all the yelling and I'm hungry and tired and Coleman wasn't good and Daddy is so mad he is staying away. And hot tears come out and so does snot and my breath goes huff because I am so glad that I am safe now and can sit with my cheek on Momma's cheek. I hear a little sniffle and I look and her eyes are teary too. I watch one water fill up and then it slides out the slanty side and down the side of her face and into her hair. Yellow hair that goes out over the plants and shines more than a leaf. She has blue eyes that are like mine even if everyone says Sticky looks more like her so when I look in her eyes it's like I can see what mine look like on my head. Same color. We checked in the bathroom mirror when I stood on the sink and she held me so I wouldn't fall and we leaned in and looked at our eyes up close. The color of our eyes is called blue but is really gray with a piece of darker blue around the outside and then lighter color in the middle. Except not as much in the middle as the black part that is a hole that I see through. Sticky has the same eyes too. Both of us have Momma's eyes in our head. And she looks at me and she doesn't wipe her tears. That is usually what she does even though she doesn't cry very many times. But she wipes tears quickly because then I can't see and maybe she hides them and no one knows the secret of crying. She is crying and she doesn't hide the secret of me crying by trying to take my tears away.

"Where's Alex?" she whispers.

"I don't know."

"Have you seen him?" Her eyes roll around in her head.

"In Coleman."

"Is he there?"

I want Momma to use her normal voice and not a whisper that sounds like she swallowed bark and to put her arms around me for a rock and hug and sing.

"Please, Anna. Look for me."

I look over at the tent. It is ripped with a big slash and so that says why Daddy yelled because he would not like a rip in the tent. Through the slash I see something moving. It is inside the tent and pushing things.

"Something is in the tent."

"What?" Momma says wispy. "What is it?"

I look more and the side of the tent pushes a bit and wiggles and a little bit of flapping. I don't know what it is inside the tent and I see Stick's little round head peeking through the rip. "Stick is playing in the tent."

"Oh, thank God." She is gaspy. "He's okay?"

"No."

"Is he hurt?"

"No; he has a poop."

"Thank God."

It is funny that she thanks God for Stick's poop. Usually she shrugs and says that he should remember to use the toilet because soon he is nearly three years old and it is a good age for in the toilet. His poop is big like a moose poop because it's too big for a diaper and yuck. But he forgets and wants a diaper. And that means he gets Momma to pick him up and snuggle. I have to go and get a clean diaper and sometimes wipes and a bag to put them in for the garbage and no snuggle at all. Momma says that he will learn when he is ready. I don't think he will because he wants all the snuggles for him. Ever.

"You need to change his diaper," I say because that is what happens next.

"No," she says and it's soft so I can barely hear.

"I will get a diaper."

"That doesn't matter."

But I know it does because it always matters.

"Is Daddy—"

"Daddy is mad."

"—there?"

"He is so mad he is staying away."

"Can you see him?"

"He told me to stay in Coleman. I did for a really long time but Stick pooped so it stinks and then the lid fell open so it wasn't—"

"It's okay," she says and closes her eyes for too long. "Listen. I need you to listen. I need you to be brave, Anna, do you hear?"

"Yes. With poop?"

"I need you to get your brother off the island. It's not safe."

"Are we going home?"

"The canoe. Drag it into the water. Take your paddle."

I don't answer. I see the blood on her neck.

"Did you see it?" she asks.

"See what?"

"A bad thing?"

"Blood."

"More than blood?"

I think and it might mean Stick's poop or that I got out of Coleman and the dark, but one of the bad things comes out of my mouth: "The black dog."

"Yes, away from the black dog."

"He's scary."

"Push off in the canoe and paddle, like I showed you."

"One, two, three, four."

"Just like that, Anna. Get your brother into the canoe and go to the middle of the lake."

"You come too."

"No. I am staying here."

"No." I shake my head.

"My neck is hurt. I can't move."

"I want to go home."

"Get into the canoe and paddle away. Wait for us."

"Can we go home?"

"Anna." She said it sharp and then a choke like her orange juice went in the wrong pipe.

"Daddy is mad," I say.

"No. You do this for Daddy. He loves you."

"So he's not mad?"

"For me. Both of us. Do you understand?"

"I want to go home."

"Go, Anna," she says in the means-it voice.

"Yes, Momma."

And the means-it voice is when I have to tidy up toys even if Sticky made them go on the floor and only some of them I did. His trucks are in the truck bin even though I didn't take them out because I don't like trucks so everybody knows they are Sticky's. Even though it is my job to put them away. The worst is when I have to look after Stick because he is my little brother and I want to play magic in the castle and all he knows is to knock it down again and again. I put the tower on the castle and he takes his fist and knocks it and he thinks that is a funny game. It is not funny and my magic fairy has no castle. I don't want to do things and the means-it voice makes me because I don't want Momma to feel mad. Not now not even ever. I am her special.

But I don't move. I crouch in and put my cheek back on Momma's because even though it isn't warm it is a smooth cheek, not wiry like Daddy's. And Gwen wants her cheek too so we both cuddle in. Her hot tears are there and Gwen sticks out her paw to wipe my momma's tear because Gwen knows that Momma doesn't want me to see her cry. Except now she doesn't seem to care. And Momma is taking breaths and she opens her eyes and looks at me and I smile because it is nice to sit and have her look at me.

"Anna, do this?"

"What?"

She closes her eyes and opens them twice. "Take your brother for a canoe ride."

"Just us?"

"It will be fun. You are big enough to paddle, right?"

"Yes." I am proud and sit up. "Are you coming too?"

"Daddy and I will follow you."

"Soon?"

"When it's time, we'll be there."

"Now?"

"We will be waiting. Daddy and I will be there."

8.

Stick is still sitting in the tent. He is on Momma's sleeping bag and his poop in his pj's stinks up.

"Come here," I say to him. "Take off those pj's."

He doesn't like his poop because he stands up and comes to the door. Usually he doesn't do what I say because he only wants to listen to Momma. I pull on the bottom of his pj's and they come down a little and the poop is inside and it makes me throw up a little bit in my mouth yuck. I pull them back up. They have ducks on them and they used to be mine but my legs got too long since I'm going to start grade one. Stick's legs are still stumpy and his knees make me laugh. They are fat circles and they don't knob out. They go straight into his legs. They tickle too and I use my hand to put a spider on his knee and make it walk around and Stick laughs.

"Ta-wick-ally," he says.

That is a very Sticky thing to say. He can't speak English

like the rest of everybody but he uses his own secret language. Momma and Daddy and me know what the words mean like that's tickle. When we meet a grown-up or we go to a party sometimes I have to tell people what Stick is saying because I speak the secret language and they don't. When we were eating Popsicles with Mrs. Buchanan and Snoopy was shut inside so he wouldn't lick Stick's face Stick's Popsicle dripped and then dropped. Mrs. Buchanan got a small bowl and put a new Popsicle inside the bowl so that Stick wouldn't drop it again. He doesn't touch Popsicles not even pink ones with his fingers because they are cold but he didn't say that. He says "I wanna werk."

Mrs. Buchanan doesn't know what a werk is and she thinks he was talking about Daddy going to work because he goes through the back gate to get his car. Stick doesn't remember going to his office so he thinks that Daddy goes and hides behind the gate all day. When Stick wants to see Daddy in the day he opens the back door and calls him. Then he thinks that Daddy stops hiding in the bushes at the end of the day and comes through the back door again. Mrs. Buchanan knows that joke so when Stick asked for a werk she thought he was talking about Daddy coming home and she said that he wouldn't for another hour or two because it was still the afternoon. I speak Stick and I know that werk is kind of like "fork" and he calls everything he eats with a werk. He doesn't say "spoon" ever.

And "copcorn" means Stick wants popcorn and anyone could guess that. When his socks are on and he wants them off and he always does in the summer, he says "My knees are stuck." That means help get my socks off and ankles and knees are mixed up. He asks for "cupper" and my momma always thinks he is asking to get in the cupboard to get a cookie but it is really supper. Momma figured it before I told her but it went on for days and days and I worried that Stick might get a cookie and I wouldn't so I hid behind the counter and waited to see. There are a lot more words that I know and other people don't. Mrs. Buchanan doesn't speak Stick and I do and so I know all that but I felt tired to explain and if I did I couldn't eat my Popsicle and I had to quick because it was summer and my Popsicle was melting. Purple and with two sticks. I got both sticks and didn't have to split because Mrs. Buchanan says I say thank you.

"Want to go on a boat ride?" I ask Sticky.

He looks at me and nods and he says "Momma."

"Come on," I say.

But he doesn't move. He sits on Momma's sleeping bag getting his old poop on it and he will get in trouble for that so I pretend I don't see because the trouble gets me too.

I want Momma. I stand up and I look over and I see her foot sitting in the plants and I don't want to go for a canoe ride even though that means I am big if I am allowed to go.

"Don't wanna," says Stick.

I stamp my bare foot and the needles don't like it. They prick me back on my little toe. My feet are standing in the mess and I don't like it. I want to make it not a mess but there is too many things to know what to do with everything. I look around and feel mad and I see a red bag. It has a big white cross on it and I know that is the Band-Aids. I am not allowed a Band-Aid unless there is blood and neither is Stick. Momma had blood and she needs a Band-Aid so I open the red bag and inside is a plastic bag that is hard to get open. I do a rip in it. That is bad because water can get in if the canoe gets tipped over. The bag isn't in the water now so maybe Daddy can fix the bag before we put it around the water. I stick my fingers in the hole and find a Band-Aid.

I'm going to take the Band-Aid for Momma for her blood. She can't get mad because that is a nice thing. I take two because there is a lot of cuts. I step over the mess and get to Momma's foot again. She is still lying down like she's on her bed but it's the plants.

"I have you a Band-Aid."

Momma doesn't answer. Her eyes are still closed and she is sleeping. I bend down and push my cheek on hers again because it is her best thing. I keep my cheek there and I don't talk and after a minute I see her eyes open. I know because I have my eye right in hers and her eyelashes give me a poke in the eyeball.

"Ow." I sit away.

"Oh, Anna," she says in a very whisper. "Be a good girl."

"I have you a Band-Aid."

She doesn't look happy or like she means thank you. I hold the two Band-Aids up to her eye so she looks at them and I start to rip the paper on one of them. It is hard to get the Band-Aid out of the paper but Momma doesn't take it from me like she does to help so I rip myself. The first rip means I can pull it and I feel happy about that.

"The canoe, Anna." She takes a really tired breath. "Please; be a good girl."

Momma closes her eyes and I put my finger on her cheek but she doesn't open up. She looks very tired and maybe like when she is sick and I am supposed to take Stick and not wake her up. We are allowed to turn on the TV even if it isn't Saturday or TV time. We can play dress-up in the closet and put on

Momma's high heels. I make Stick wear the black ones because the red are the best and shiny. I think of Stick in my daddy's tie and my momma's black high heels with his dingle sticking out because he was naked but I also think of the black dog too and my tummy feels shaky.

"Momma. Mom?"

She looks mad.

There is a bad sniff in the air and I don't like it. It makes my tummy feel more shaky and I think the bacon ball from Stick's mouth again and I'd like to sniff Gwen. She isn't in my hand. I look over and see Stick is sitting in the door of the tent. He is holding Gwen and I don't like it too.

"Sticky!" I stomp so that he knows I am mad and I grab Gwen from him. It is easy because his arms are fat and not muscle and I get Gwen and sniff to make sure she is still right. Stick tries to grab her back, but I stand up and hold her over my head so he can't reach. I want Momma to come and get him away because Gwen is mine. I look over and see her foot standing in the plants and she wants me to get Stick in the canoe. If I can do that I am her strong girl and Daddy will come back to be in the family even though it's not my fault and I can make it better if I am a super good girl and I am.

"Come on, Sticky," I say still holding Gwen away.

"No."

I take a few steps toward the canoe. "Come on."

"Gimme." He points to Gwen.

I will never but I look over and Momma is there. I hold Gwen because I am trying to do what Momma says.

"You want Gwen? Come to the canoe."

Stick's eyes open up and he thinks he is really lucky. And then his eyes go more shut because he knows I never ever give him Gwen and maybe he will come and get her and get a punch instead. I would like to punch him because I am mad at Momma for making me take him for a canoe. Stick makes a lot of trouble for me and I get in trouble instead of him. I feel mad and I'm not going to give him Gwen. No way. I pull her back and sniff and Stick sits back down in the door of the tent because he knows he won't get his fat hands on Gwen. He can't even say her name right. When I tell him to say her name he says "Glen" and I tell him wrong and he forgot the word "w." He says "Wind" and that is wrong too.

Stick's bum is back on Momma's sleeping bag and I won't get it off even though Momma said. I kick at the floor and my toe hits something. Ow. It's the tin. And I pick it up and know that it's the cookie tin and it now has a bunch of holes in the top and it has a bang and it must have been Stick trying to get a cookie. I look up and he is watching me and I know that he really wants a cookie because his little tongue pokes out of his mouth and he licks his lips. I shake the tin.

"Cookie?"

He nods his head yes.

"Come on." I hold the tin out and shake it and start walking back to the water. I am calling him like I call Snoopy, holding the treat out and making my voice squeaky because it sounds not like me and more like a girl who is nice. "Come here."

Stick stands up and puts one foot in the mess. He has to step to get around some eggs that are broken and a jar of jam that has the top on. Lucky. If the top was off Stick would have stopped to stick his fingers in it and lick. He likes the wax part that is on the top and he and I get to trade who gets to lick it when it comes off a new jar that is opened up for the first time. He knows he can't get the jar open so I see him look at the jam but I shake the cookies again.

"Here, Sticky." I call him like Snoopy.

He knows it is my Snoopy voice because he sticks his tongue out and puts his hands up near his chest and curls them like paws. Stick likes Snoopy and got jealous because Snoopy and I play and so Stick made an inside dog that lives in his head.

"Woof," he barks.

"Good boy, Stick. Come on."

He keeps walking and I go backwards and then my heel hits the canoe and it makes thump on the metal. Ow.

I look at the canoe. It is half in the water floating and half on a piece of dirt that turns into the water. There is also Daddy's paddle lying in the dirt. I think eek because I see that it is broken. The long handle part is cracked in half and he will be so so mad. Momma gave him the paddle from Santa and a man made it exactly right. So so mad. I didn't break it and I will need a paddle and I grab the side of the canoe to push it in with one hand. The canoe won't move. It feels like when I put my hands on our car when it is in the driveway and try to push. I can't lift or push the car and Daddy says that most people can't. Even a big man. He says that sometimes small people have moved cars when they want to save someone like Superman. He gets special powers and can move things that they couldn't before. I close my eyes and think about a laser beam coming to my forehead and the special powers flow into my head and they laser down to my chest and out my arms and legs and I take a big breath and I push.

Nothing happens. The canoe is too stuck for special powers

even. Daddy pulled it up enough so that it won't float away. He should come and help.

"Daddy!" I say.

He doesn't call back to tell me one minute and he doesn't come. I have to ask Momma to do most things and I look up and am about to tell her to come and get the canoe out and I see a foot. Stick starts barking in my face and he has his hands on the tin and he pulls it. I tell him to go away and I try and push the canoe with my leg but it is stuck. I push Stick back and try again but no. It is stuck and I need Daddy. When I push with Daddy it slips on the sand. Stick falls and goes plop on the sand on his bum and then he looks mad. Like when he got stung by a bee and his face went all red and twisty. He yells and stands up again and tackles me. He wants the tin. I throw Gwen in the canoe so she won't get ripped. He grabs the tin and turns to run away. His legs take many steps but I only have to take two and I have my arms around him and my chin over his head. His foot sticks out the back and he gets it tangled between mine and we fall. The tin is the hot potato except that we both want it and it's under Sticky's belly on the ground so I have to flip him and grab it back. I get it in my hands and go back to the canoe and he comes and tries to grab it again. He is mad and not crying but growling and yelling.

I hold the tin up above my head. I still need it to make him do things. He won't stop and he gets his claws out and scratches my face hard. Stick is small but he can be mean and I am not supposed to be too rough but he doesn't care. I scream because it feels like blood on my cheek and I jump up with the tin up high and he is still clawing. He is hurting me and I shout at him to stop and he doesn't so I throw the tin. He keeps clawing me because he doesn't know that I'm not holding the tin and I hear clang clang clang and it stops us both. We look and the tin has gone into the front of the canoe in front of Momma's seat. Stick shoves me back and grabs the edge of the canoe. I know he wants the cookies and doesn't care but my face hurts and I put my hand on the scratch. Stick puts his belly on the side of the canoe and flops his head inside. He pulls on the bar and slides on his belly and the canoe nearly tips but it doesn't and only his body tips inside. His head is on the ground and his legs plop in after but he doesn't care because all he cares about is cookies. He gets up and steps over my bar and walks back up to Momma's seat. He sits and keeps the back of his head to me and I see he has the tin in his hands and he is trying to open it. I don't care because my cheek hurts and my feelings hurt too. I have my hand on the canoe. I feel my hand on the canoe move up into the air a little bit.

And wait a minute the canoe is loose on the sand and I can take a step forward and it comes with me and the canoe is swimming. Stick's bum in the back made the front float up from the dirt. I get excited because I got the canoe in the water and I didn't think I could and I didn't even need Daddy or Momma to help. Stick sits in Momma's seat and wrestles with the cookies and can't get them open and I try and get my leg up over the side of the canoe. I can't because now the canoe is swimming, it is high up. I can pull it easily and see a rock like Momma showed me. I pull the canoe to the rock and Stick doesn't care because all he thinks is cookie cookie cookie. I step on the rock and it is a good choice of rock because it isn't a slippy and my foot sticks to it. I step over the side and into the middle like I should so it's not tippy. My pj pants pull down and my bum smile is out so I have to reach and pull them up. The canoe wiggles but not much and we float a little and I look at the water and remember no paddle. I don't have a life jacket on and that is trouble. I look for a yellow spot and there is no life jacket on the floor and I need a paddle. I look back at the sand and a paddle is lying there. I think it is two paddles but it is one and broken. Daddy's paddle is broken I remember. So so mad.

"Open," says Stick.

He gives me a smile and I know he wants to be friends with me because he can't open the tin. He has a hand on the tin and a fat finger is trying to scrape the side to get it open. It makes me remember the raccoon that comes and gets our garbage. It can open all the tins and even the wood box that my dad puts all the garbage inside of and forgets to lock. Sometimes the raccoon hides inside the box and waits for my daddy to come early in the morning when he is still half asleep and has a whiskery face and no glasses. Daddy opens the box and the raccoon jumps out and says boo and I look out the window and watch the raccoon run away with a black mask on his face and I can see that he is laughing about his joke of scaring Daddy. Another time when I watched the raccoon open up all the garbage I got in trouble for not saying but the raccoon was very good at our garbage. He had little fingers that got into everything and when he needed to open a lid he could use a fingernail to push it in and make a hole and pull and eat everything inside. There are holes in the cookie tins but Stick's fingernails won't fit in them to pull. Even though I am at the other end of the canoe I can see that Stick would do better with hands like a raccoon's. His hands look fat and like they can't do anything.

"Open," he says.

I just sit there because the canoe is long and tippy and it doesn't seem like I have energy to get all that way.

"Open now."

Stick is trying to pretend he is the boss but he isn't. He is using his Daddy voice and making his eyebrows push up in the middle like that is going to make me move. I want a cookie too maybe but I am tired and there is some wind that makes my hair blow and it feels a little bit like Momma's fingers so I don't want to move from my spot.

"Nana. Open, Nana."

I look over the edge. The canoe is made of metal and it is the color of a money if the money wasn't a shiny one but older and with a beaver. Or like the one that my grandpa gave me with the head of a guy that I don't know him. The edge of the canoe moves up and down a little or the water is moving up and down like a rocking and that feels nice too. The sun is smiling down and the water twinkles hello when they touch. My eyes twinkle back and that is nice and I ignore Stick who is huffy at the other end of the canoe. I stare at the water and it ripples all over like the skin of a fish except more like a sandbar except not the color of sand but smooth glitters like a fish. And maybe a hundred fish are swimming just under the top of the water and they are all having their backs up against the top so I can see them moving along the water and flowing under the canoe and Stick and I will be picked up in the canoe and we will ride on the backs of the fish. And they will take us to their fish castle that has a queen fish who is bigger than everyone else and she will welcome us and give us chocolate to say hi and after that maybe some chocolate milk too.

But in the fish land we can't breathe in water so there are bubbles all around and a fish puts a bubble on my lips with its nose and when that bubble is done another fish comes and brings a new bubble. I say thank you and I'm not sure if it's the same fish that brought the bubble before so it is a good idea to say thank you anyway when you aren't sure because it never hurts anyone. The fish says you are welcome and dips his fish nose at me and I think that the fish seem to want manners so saying thank you might get me more treats. Fish don't like bubble gum.

A big grape bubble goes flying out my mouth and the fish gets whacked on the nose and all of a sudden all the fish turn to look at me so I pull out my magic wand and whack whack whack. The battle of the fish means I have to keep fighting and magic-wanding the fish. And the battle gets bigger and an octopus that is my friend comes to help and he has many arms and they all start going whack whack whack so many times and it's enough that the canoe starts to wiggle because all the fish are growing big teeth to get us and opening their mouths. The edge of the canoe goes dip and I see the fish are trying to tip us into the water so there will not be bubbles to breathe so I must magic-wand more! I yell "Charge" and say the spell that is the strongest magic spell and I hear a big clang and it is electric from my magic spell but I hear a roll and look across the canoe and that's when I see Stick is standing up.

Stick is picking up the cookie tin after he dropped it and it went clank. He tucks it under his arm and he has moved on his bum like he is supposed to but now he is at the bar and is standing and trying to get a leg over it and hold onto the tin both at the same time.

"Sit, Stick," I say because I trained his inside dog with tricks.

He doesn't care. He won't listen with the inside dog and just wants to get over the bar so I can open the cookies and he can eat them all. I don't want him to eat them all and that is not fair. He gets one leg over the bar but it is hard to stand with holding the cookies too. He falls back a little and pulls his body up and then falls because his head is so big like a basketball and it pulls him over all the time. The cookies go clank on the canoe and Stick's head goes crack on the edge and I think uh-oh that's going to be bloody. I look at the edge for the blood and I see the water is there and the fish army. There are no fish but the water is right at the edge and Stick is in a ball on the bottom and one of his legs is hooked up on the bar and the other is not. We are tipsy.

I put both my hands out on the other side. Both my hands are on the edge of the canoe and I spread my knees wide out and hang my head over. I keep my hips still but we wiggle the other way and I lean. This is what Momma made me do when she would sit in the canoe and try to make it tipsy. I would stop it by holding still and she would try again and again and she is bigger so after a lot of times we could tipsy into the water and be wet and she grabs me and we laugh.

"Sit, Stick," I say in the Daddy voice and push my eyebrows in the middle.

I look over and he is crying and still in a pile.

"Get to the middle," I say.

It's one of the biggest rules in our family. When Daddy and Momma are pushing the canoe and Momma steers from the back and Daddy is the power at the front and Stick and I have to sit in the middle. I get to sit on Coleman because I am better at not wiggling and being higher up and Stick sits on the bag with our clothes that is squishy so sometimes I wish I sat there because

Stick always gets the good things. But really I like the back most times because Momma will talk to me in a quiet voice. We can have our fishing rods in the water and even I can play with Lego but there is no standing up if we want to stay in the middle.

I lean out and look at water and then smack the water comes up to my face. I jump back and grab the other side of the edge and I put my knees out and we tipsy that way so far my fingers are in so I jump into the middle and we rock to one side and the other and I look down and away and see that Stick has rolled into the middle like a good boy. His leg is still up on the bar but he is on his back and his pj's are all wet because now he is lying in water that got in the canoe. My face is wet too. And my fingers. I wait until the canoe isn't tipsy.

"Stay, Stick," I say.

"Okey."

"Good dog."

Stick sticks out his tongue but he doesn't really play.

I can see red bang on the side of Stick's head but not blood. He has a bang and he looks sad lying on his back with his foot in the air and in the water that is on the bottom of the canoe. I keep my hands on both edges and move in to see him and the cookie tin is floating by. I grab it. The water covers my foot only and there is no tin can with the label peeled off and it used to have tomatoes that we can use to get the water out of the boat. I help Stick up and the back of his hair is sopping wet but hangs onto the water and goes like a white fin at the back of his head.

"I am the queen and magic and you are in the fish army," I say.

"Fishie."

"Okay?"

Stick nods and he is staring at the cookie tin and thinks I might take it away. I get my fingers on it and it is slippy and wet and I kind of wish I had claws so I could stick one in the hole that is in the top that wasn't there before when we left the cottage. I snuck a cookie when Momma wasn't looking. She found the lid off when I forgot to put it back because the cookie was so good I had to eat it right away. She looked at the lid off to the side and put it back. She looked at me and smiled and said "A bear must have gotten into our cookie tin." And I smiled too and shrugged my shoulders so she wouldn't know. I get the lid off and whoa the smell of cookies and there are chocolate chips and I stuff one into my mouth and take another and give one to Stick. Finally he is eating a cookie and he is quiet and we are sitting in ankle water in the canoe with sopping wet bums.

9.

I eat a lot of cookies and my stomach feels a little sick. I turn and look back at the island. The sand has moved away. There are little waves that are pushing us and the wind is still in the air. The canoe is floating. I need Momma's paddle to make us go really fast back to the island.

"Canoe ride all done, Stick."

"Yep."

I want to get back to the island to be with Momma and then Daddy comes back. I look for the paddle that is Momma's that she was using in the back to make Js to keep the canoe straight. It is a golden paddle with leather on the handle to make it soft for her hands. There is a guy that looks like an eagle on the flat part that goes in the water and she says that it is made to be like an otter's tail because they are really good at pushing water and swimming. Momma's paddle makes our canoe swim straight.

Daddy's paddle is tall like him and Momma told him how to

do it. It has a really really long tail and is more like yellow. Stick and I have dinky paddles that are the same even though I am the oldest and soon I will get a bigger paddle that this man with a funny name made. Kettlewell. Everyone will be so proud that I am so big and can make the canoe go fast. I look and there are no paddles in the canoe. I forgot. They are on the island with Momma and I want to see her. I did what she said and Stick and I have been for a canoe ride so now I will go back and see her and Daddy will be there too. And get life jackets because I forgot. We can all get in the canoe with the life jackets and paddles and Coleman and we can go home. My bum is wet and I've had enough camping now so home is better. I remember my bed, which is my favorite place and I can't wait to get inside and I reach over to get Gwen and she is floating but her hair is wet. She is heavier than she normally is. I feel sad because I don't like Gwen to change and the sniff is not the same. I give Sticky one more cookie and tell him that his stomach will feel kind of sick too but he doesn't listen. He takes a cookie in his other hand and starts to nibble. I put the lid back on the cookie tin and put it down so it can float around wherever it wants.

I will have to paddle with my hands to get the paddles to paddle and it's funny. I tell Stick to stay in the middle of the canoe.

"Okey."

I wiggle up to the pointy front of the canoe that is Daddy's seat and put my chest on it like my momma showed. There is air blowing that is pushing my hair back and mostly my hair hangs down the front with bangs and a little bit sometimes in my eyes. Momma cuts it with special scissors that Daddy can't use to cut Stick's noodles because they are only for bangs. Now my bangs is pushed back by wind and I feel them go to the side not like Jessica's bangs at my school who has pigtails. I want my hair not like that but like Jessica's with shiny bangs so I put my hand to push it forward and it blows back. Jessica's hang forward and shiny because her mom puts hot air on them and a brush that is a circle and it pulls shinies into bangs with a spray that is not like water. It makes my tongue feel like a sour key candy and when it went in my mouth my tongue wanted to get up and crawl away. I put my hand in my bangs again and now they are wet with water and only half hanging. Not like Jessica's. At all.

I lean in and use both hands to make cups. The water feels nice. My hands look white in the water. White and wiggling and the small chopper waves lick at them. Yum. And I pull once and look up and the sand is closer now and it is working to paddle with my hands not a paddle.

I will fix the paddle before Daddy comes back and I can give it to him and it's just like when he came to the cottage. I lean forward and stick my hands in and pull pull pull lots of times. The water is floating by the canoe so I think it is swimming forward and I pull more and my hair gets pushed back a little from my forehead but the girls with the pigtails. Jessica isn't here so she can't see and laugh so I keep pulling. My arms at the top start to get burn and so does my back. I have to stop and put my chest down on the tippy point of the canoe and let the burn drip out my fingertips. It slides down my arms and goes so I can pull water again. I pull pull pull and I turn my head to the side so my whole hand can be in the water and pulling like Momma says to do with the paddle to make it go faster. I look at the island and a tree on it and it is getting a little closer so I keep pulling as much as I can. Soon the burn comes again and I have to stop and drip.

I need help and I turn to ask Stick if he will paddle. He is sitting in the middle of the canoe like I told him and not moving because he is busy eating the cookie I gave him. He eats it slow because he always eats anything with chocolate really slow so he will have some in the end and I won't. I feel mad that he is eating every cookie and not me.

"Help me?"

He looks up and holds up half a cookie and has chocolate smeared on his face just to show that he has a cookie left and I don't. He pushes his round cheeks into smiles. He has two dots in them. Momma said when he paddles he only dips for lilies and doesn't make the canoe swim any faster or maybe even slows it down. When she said that she and I had a giggle that Stick couldn't see but not like a mean laugh. It was a laugh because the Stick is pretty funny and also still like a baby a lot of the time so you can't ask him to do hard things and then get mad because he forgets or wanders off or doesn't. Stick is like having an extra bag. Except a bag sits still and holds clothes. This bag is wet and eating all the cookies and showing me he has some when I have none.

"Cookie!" says Stick.

I look at Daddy's broken paddle on land and worry drips into my heart. I don't see Daddy. Momma said to take Stick in the canoe and wait. A little puddle of black sits in my heart too and I know Momma said to wait. I am supposed to get Stick in the canoe and wait and now I am going back. I am bad. I want to be good girl and Daddy will come back again and my family will be four.

"Wanna go for a ride, Stick?"

"Yep."

I am a good girl.

I scoop my hands in the water a lot of times but I can't turn the canoe around. I don't know what to do and worry that I am bad again. I look at the canoe and think what Momma said that a canoe is the same pointy on both sides. I need to climb around to where the back is pointing and I can go that way. Only it will be hard not to be tipsy. I put my hands on the sides of the canoe and move my feet. I am in the middle with only a little tipsy and I have to step over the cookies and step over Stick and his crumbs. I am at the back of the canoe and it is now the front. I lean on the pointy part and put my chest on it. I put my hands like cups and I pull pull pull and Stick and I go into the lake and I keep going. My arms hurt and I do more pulls. I keep going and after a long time maybe forever I think that my stomach feels cookie sick and that the canoe is going rock rock rock like a lullaby. I am tired because Coleman wouldn't let me sleep so much. The wind pushes at my hair and my arms feel so heavy from the burn and it won't drip out the ends of my fingers because now it's too thick and so it just stays still and I try to keep pulling. I know Momma feels really proud.

Part II

Mainland near Lake Opeongo,
Algonquin Park, 1991

10.

I open my eyes and I am dreaming that I am in a tin can like a little fish. I am dreaming except I can see. Momma has clean toes and her foot is in a sandal that is leather and wraps around her toe. I curl my arm around her brown leg and it is so smooth. I rub her skin and she rings the doorbell of Jessica's house and pushes my hand away and bends her neck to smile at me. Her forehead is smooth like a bowl and her teeth are a piano but not the black keys just the white. She has a very pretty dress and I feel proud that she is my momma and that Jessica gets to see. Momma doesn't have a job because she wants to be with me and so we go to the park and music and then sometimes playdates when we want friends to be with us only sometimes not always. The door opens and plaid shorts with hairy legs are standing.

Steven's voice says come in. Steven is Jessica's daddy and he is the parent at home. I am supposed to say "Hi, Steven" and that is hard. Momma gives me a push and that means manners. Jessica is on the stairs and she has a doll in her hand. Barbie! It is a Barbie I haven't met. I try to see Barbie and Jessica runs into the kitchen and I can't see her anymore. Momma giggles and I look and she is gone and so is Jessica but only Barbie is on the ground. I go to pick her up and she disappears into fairy dust when I touch her. Now I can't see and I feel around and it's only metal and I don't know what it is.

Maybe a can like the one that holds tuna fish or one that Daddy opened and the fish were lying next to each other like a sleepover yuck. The fish in the cans have backbones and even sometimes heads and I do too because I can see through my eyes.

There is breathing. It goes in and out and in and out. And something touches my foot. Small and pointy. I jump up. Bang my head goes clang. Ouch. I look up and see the tippy point of the canoe is above me. I am down on the ground of the canoe and I slid under the seat. It's wet around me. I pull my feet in and water goes slosh. I look over to see what touched me and there is Stick's gobby head. It is big like the moon. I can tell that he was sleeping because his eyes are smooshed on a little. I can see the line of the canoe where it is sewed together with metal stitches has made a print on his face.

"Cookie?" he asks.

I am in the canoe. Stick has the tin and he has shuffled to my end of the canoe. His nose makes the breath. I sit up and keep my hands on either side of the edges to make sure we don't take a fall in the water by mistake because a canoe is tipsy. The sky is blue and it is a little cold and I look to the side and see there is big long grass that has its feet stuck into the water beside the canoe. Then there are sticks that are crisscrossed all over each

other in a hump like the back of a turtle. I blink and I don't
know where I am and then I think camping and then I know I
took Stick for a canoe ride for a long time. Maybe we are back
again and I look to see if I know and it doesn't look the same. It's
not a turtle's shell that is beside the canoe. It is sticks and some
mud with parts that have grass growing out. Our canoe is lying
beside it and so is less tipsy but I don't like that Stick is moving
around inside the canoe. It makes me scared of getting wetter.

"Let's get out," I say.

"Cookie?"

I grab the tin from him. Stick screams.

I try to stand and my one leg feels like someone has chopped
it off by accident or on purpose. It won't move for a minute and
I think that the water at the bottom of the canoe has ruined it.
It feels like a piece of meat and then my foot is like Daddy's
sneaker. And then it hurts and I grab it and think ouch and then
it goes prickle and a cactus is rolling up and down except there
is no cactus in the canoe. I want to get out to get away from the
cactus because it hurts my leg so I chuck the cookie tin onto the
turtle's stick shell that is beside the canoe and get my hands on
the edges. I step right out onto the sticks with the leg that still
walks. My pj's are a waterfall for a minute and then they go drip
on the canoe. Drip drip drip it sounds like a clock. The clock
stops when I step up to the sticks. They feel pricky too but not
as much. I find a good place for my foot and then move the
dead one out and crouch down to hold the side of the canoe like
Momma would.

"Come on, Stick," I say, making my voice high like a momma.
"Step out."

Stick nods and he is staring at the cookie tin. He stands up and it's hard to hold the edge of the canoe because of his big bum and the canoe rocks but I hold it. He puts his hand on my shoulder and grabs one of the sticks and pulls up but it is tricky because his bum is so heavy. It is even harder because his bum is wet too. Water drips off in a stream and then drop drop drop. I hang onto the canoe as hard as I can and he manages to get his bum up and out.

"Ow," he says with his fat feet on the sticks.

I grab the tin and look over and see we can get to the earth if we step off the turtle and along the sticks where there is earth.

"Come on." I shake the tin.

"Cookie," he says.

I take a few steps and ow. I don't like walking on sticks and I feel yuck and my heart goes boom because I think where is Gwen? I look over and she is floating in the canoe. She is look-ing at the sky. I can tell that she thinks that I have left her and I will never be back to snuggle and she is all alone.

"Gwen." I drop the tin clang and hop ouch back over to the canoe. I grab the edge and pull it close and reach but she floats away to the other side. I need a grown-up to hold the canoe or I need longer arms like Daddy.

"Daddy!" I yell and look around.

I can't see him and I feel mad because it's an emergency. He is gone and so I need to do some jobs myself that I didn't used to do but this is one that I need help.

"Momma!"

No one comes and all the parents are mad and gone away and I am not supposed to scream except for an emergency and it is because the canoe is pushing away from the stick turtle so I grab it back. It bumps against the turtle and the turtle must feel angry because it kicks the canoe back and it starts to get away again and I see Gwen floating all alone and so I jump.

I land and splash into the ankle water in the canoe and my hand is on soggy Gwen but then we keep going. Crack my nose goes into the canoe and it feels like blood. The crack comes from electric in my eyes and I grab Gwen and we roll. Bang on my head and I am pushed in the water and my pj's pull me down. My whole body is under the water and I can't breathe because I didn't get to count before going in and bubbles blow out of my mouth and there are no more and I feel water has pushed so far up my nose it is in my brain. It soaks up all the water. It is so heavy I am pulled down and I thrash my feet and I hug Gwen close. I can't swim because of the water in my head and I might be falling down or up. There are stars or white dots going round and making me dizzy. I am too tired and my swimming doesn't work and I kick once but I can't anymore.

But then something hits my hip and it keeps me up and I know a dolphin has come to save me with its nose. It will push me up onto a rock or I can ride on its back so we can travel but I can still breathe. But the dolphin doesn't push it just keeps its nose there and I must be lying across the body because I seem to be keeping in the air and my nose can breathe. I hold Gwen up so her nose can breathe too. Then I look at my arm out of the water and I see that I did not fall into a deep lake. I am sitting on the earth under the water. My bum is on the ground. I bend my waist and my head is up in the sky. I take in big gulps of air and it makes me cough. Gooey snot runs out my nose. I wipe with my sleeve and no one tells me not to. I get my feet down. The water is up to the tops of my legs. I stand up quickly because the water is bad. The ground is mucky muck. I put my feet down and they sink in. Yucky muck.

Behind me the dolphin has died. It rescued me with its last breath like I am the powerful queen or maybe a magic one and a fairy with big magic not small dust. The dolphin rolled over and is lying on the muck beside me except it's the canoe's belly. I didn't recognize the canoe's belly seeing it for the first time but that's what it is. It slowly rolls back like it is just waking up from a nap. The tippy point is full of dirt and there is brown mucky water inside. It's like a bathtub after a bath when I was really dirty from playing soccer in the mud and I rolled to get a kick but it didn't work. Instead I went squishing through the mud and it went up my pants and came out in the bathtub and my daddy said "Holy cow" when he looked because he didn't know that a girl could ever be that dirty. I felt proud because I am.

The mud tries to drink my feet down. I pull a foot out and pull the other foot out and the first one sinks in again. I give Gwen a sniff but she is all wet. I give her a squeeze and she cries out the water and I say "Don't worry, Gwen, I will save you." So I pull a foot out and put it closer to the side and then pull another foot out and put it even closer to the side. Gwen gets to the side of the water that is grass and mud and I hold her close. My knees come up and I sit and let my head fall down. I put my holes where my eyes go on my knees and let them sit in there. Gwen and I are close and it is dark with my knees in my eyes so I don't have to see. I sit and stay like that and Gwen keeps her cheek on mine.

I don't move until I hear a soft jingle. I look up and know it is the cookie tin. Stick is sitting on the stick turtle beside the dirty bathtub canoe. He is sitting on the sticks with the tin in between his feet and his stupid fat hands are trying to get the lid off the tin but they can't. I see that the sticks and mud make a sidewalk between us. I stand up and pick over the sticks to get to where he is sitting. The sticks get more ouch as I get closer because there are more of them and less mud. But I get to Stick and he looks at me like he is sad that my hands are less stupid than his.

"Come on," I say.

I grab the tin out of his hands and he yowls but stands up and I take one of his hands and pull on it. I keep pulling and he comes on across the sticks to the earth.

"Owey, owey," he says as he walks.

The sticks jab at our feet and we have to go so slow because his legs are stumpy. I get more sticks in my feet because I am going first. If we hopped it would be faster or skipped. He can't and I can but he is hugging my hand with his so I wait. We get our feet on the dirt and it feels better. I keep his hand and we go to a place up a little from the water that is drier but that doesn't matter because our pj's are sopping. We sit and I open the tin and I give one to me and one to Stick and eat a cookie.

After a minute I hear smack smack smack. I think it is Stick's lips because he is eating a lot of cookies but it is not. Someone is swimming in the lake in front of us. Smack smack smack and huff breathing like Stick's nose as it swims. I think a rat because I can see the fur but it swims more and I remember looking underneath the water that was like a fish tank at the zoo and it's a beaver. I hold Gwen up to look at the beaver and its tail smacks again and she swims around in a circle and makes a breath on the water like swimming isn't hard but she is mad at us. We eat more cookies each until all the cookies are gone and I look out at the lake. The beaver comes making a circle again. I think maybe the pile of sticks are her house and she doesn't like us there. She smacks her tail on the water again and Stick looks at me.

"It's a beaver. She says hi," I tell him because I don't want him to feel like she is mad.

Stick smiles and looks back at Beaver swimming and holds up his hand. "Hi, Beaver."

She smacks back. Stick thinks she is waving but I think she doesn't like us much and wants us to go away and no one wants us here. The parents are both mad and not coming not just Daddy this time it is different. The sun gives too much shine and there are trees everywhere with their dark in between and I don't see anything I know.

11.

Momma said to me "Daddy and I will be there." I am a
good girl and our family is four. I don't want to wait here because I don't like it but I am supposed to watch Stick when
Momma is not here. I am not old enough to be a babysitter because that is a girl who has long hair and her jeans go loose
around her shoe and nail polish that is pink like a pink Popsicle
except dark. I want nail polish but Momma says no and I can't
babysit yet so I just watch Stick. I don't know how long until
Momma and Daddy come.

   I look at Stick and he is boring to watch and I wish that Gwen
could sniff like when she is dry and in my bed and we are in
a cozy snuggle under the blankets. She is wet and her fur is
mussed up. I hold her arm and twist it and water drips out of
her. I worry her stuffing will drip. I check her for holes like once
when the part by her neck came loose. White fluff came out and
I showed Momma that Gwen's stuffing was coming out of her

body and I knew she would die. Momma said no she wouldn't die and that we needed to needle her up. We got a pricky needle and got string that was brown. We had dark brown but that wouldn't hide on Gwen so we went to the store and then to Mrs. Buchanan's house and then she had string that was just like Gwen. I held Gwen and Momma got the string through the end of the needle that had a surprise teeny tiny hole at the very tip. Momma stitched up Gwen and I held her and said that it would be okay because her stuffing would stay in. I look at the part on her neck and it still works.

And so Gwen is good but she doesn't sniff as good. I see a rock a little bit over and stand up. The rock is smooth and flat and a little away from the water like the ones we use to dry socks. I put my hand on the rock and it is warm but not hot and the sun is coming more so soon it will get hot. I stretch Gwen out on the rock and she looks happy. I stand in the sun and then I feel like Gwen too. I reach down and my pj's can also cry out water when I bunch them up on my leg. I would like not to be in wet pj's and I take off the top and the bottom. I twist them like Momma does and lie them on the rock.

I hear nose breathing and Stick is behind me trying to take off his pj's too. He copies me always. If I eat cake then he wants cake. I have a doll with pretty eyes and he wants it. I play with the smaller Lego that is for big girls and he doesn't want his big Lego for babies but wants my small Lego for big girls. He has his pj top off but just part of the arms and the body of it is still over his head and he can't lift up higher because his elbows are stuck.

"Help, help," he says.

I stand beside him and lift the shirt up and it comes up but then gets stuck. I pull more and it goes up from his neck and I can see his chin and his cheeks and his mouth sticking out but it is stuck around his head. He pulls his arms down so they come out but his big head is stuck in the circle and I can't get it off the top.

"Get it off!"

"I'm trying," I say and I bunch all the extra pj at the top and pull up because I am taller but not tall enough and it is hard to pull when he has such a big head.

"Get off."

He is mad at me now and I know that he needs a smaller head and not one like a rock. I pull and nothing. The rock head is stuck in the pj's. And that gives me an idea and I step back to stand up on the rock and tell him to move closer. He can't see and his arms are out and his white round belly is hanging out and it makes me laugh. The pj's cover his eyes and he trips on his feet around the ground with his arms out. I laugh again because it's like we are playing Marco Polo.

"Say Marco," I tell him.

He doesn't say Marco. He doesn't go to birthday parties yet so he doesn't know that you say Marco and everyone answers Polo and even though it is dark under the blindfold you can hear where people are and try to find them. Except sometimes I can peek under the bottom of the blindfold if it is tied up on my nose and I can tilt my head under but not too much so the peeking is still a secret. And we play hot potato and you pass the potato around and pretend it's hot even though it isn't really hot and when the music stops everyone points at the person who is stuck holding the potato and I feel really bad. My cheeks feel like hot potatoes and someone says they are pink. Jessica's mother told me not to peek but I still did because it was too dark and

I wanted to not be "it" so I could get out from the dark. I don't like to be "it."

"Get me out," Stick yells.

He didn't say please but I reach and pull his arm closer to the rock so I can reach. I am taller on the rock and he is only up to my belly button so I can get the sleeves and the end of the top all together and I pull straight up and pop. The circle comes off Stick's face and he has a red line on his nose from the neck.

"Stop growing your head," I say.

"Stop it," he says and he doesn't speak much English but he wants to say that he is mad.

I think Stick has English inside his head and he doesn't make it come out loud so much even when it comes out the wrong way or backwards like my name Nana. His words are in his head and they get stuck when they swim around inside. This is because I saw a picture of a brain and there are little squiggly paths that wind around and around like worms and English has to travel through the squiggles that are like tunnels for worms. A baby can't push their thinking because there are so many worms. Stick isn't a baby anymore but he still is wormy gross and I tease him about worms and get in trouble when I put them in his face. I have to put them back in the dirt to let them have a nice life again. And if I chopped there would be two worms instead of one and they could go one to the house and one to the alley. That is two worms having a nice life but I still don't like worms and not in my head but I will touch them sometimes if it makes Stick say yuck.

Now Stick is wiggling and trying to get out of his pj bottoms just like me. I tell him to sit and I grab the elastic at the top and pull so that they come inside out and off. They get stuck at the last part of his feet. I sit down to get a better grip and he thinks I am not pulling anymore.

"My knees are stuck," he says.

"Ankles, silly," and I know it is Stick speak and sit and pull them off.

It is easy to get them off his feet not like his head and I remember the poo almost too late but it isn't there anymore. Or I can see a few patches but they are mostly gone and any bigger chunk is not there. That is good because those are what I hate and smell the worst. Stick's pj bottoms do smell a little and I wouldn't want them on my nose but far away it isn't so bad. He rolls over and gets onto his knees and says "Ouch" on the ground and gets on his feet. He puts his feet down and his bum is in my face. He bends and I can see a red starfish and if I looked I would see right up Sticky's bum. Yuck. Once when Sticky didn't have on diapers and he bent down and we saw up his bum even if we didn't mean to look because it was right there in our face. Daddy said that we could probably see all the secrets of the universe in there. I peek and no. And Daddy was wrong. There are no secrets just a little bit of poo.

I twist his pj's like I twisted mine and I put them on the rock on the other side of Gwen. I spread them out so the arms and legs are straight and after a minute it looks like Stick is lying on the rocks and so am I. And our pj's are the same with ducks on them so it looks like two kids are lying on the rock except one is bigger than the other just like I am bigger than Stick. He comes up to my chest when we are standing except when I am standing on the rock and then only up to my belly button. I think his head might already be as big as mine but I hope it won't grow anymore or else he will get stuck in his pj top forever.

My skin feels warm now that my pj's are off and I put my arms up to the sky. We are supposed to wait for our parents and it is okay because the sun is smiling on me and it feels nice. I let my feet wiggle around because the cookies have sprinkled sugar down into my toes. I hop on a foot and my bottom skin hits crunchy dirt. I see a little more sand a few feet over and closer to the water and I step and it feels really nice and soft on my feet. I let my feet jiggle more and my hands wave around and I laugh because it is fun and then Stick comes over too. He jumps and waves his hands like me because he doesn't know how to dance other than jiggle up and down on the spot. My momma has to dance for him by taking his hands in hers or sometimes putting him on her hip so her legs are the ones dancing for him. If my daddy is dancing too I can step on his toes. He holds my arms and his shoes are shiny and black and slippery but if I balance just right and wear my sneakers not socks then I can stay on for the ride. But now Sticky is dancing like I am dancing and I look at him and he laughs with his face all bunched up in a smile and his small teeth are showing and the two dimples on each side. He puts his arms up like me and waves them around. I put a foot out and he puts a foot out. I wave my hand hard and he waves his hand hard. I put my thumb on my nose to do a na-na-na-boo-boo and he does it too. I stick out my tongue and blah blah blah.

"Naked naked naked," I say and I wiggle my bum.

He laughs even harder and wiggles his bum and his dingle wiggles too but it is such a shrinky dink that it doesn't wiggle so much. So I wiggle my bum more. "Bum bum bum."

"Bum," he says laughing.

I know I can make Stick laugh and laugh and it is like I am

doing a job like a babysitter now because he is having fun. I start going in a circle and then I pretend to fall which is his most favorite and I go sideways in the sand and make it look like a cartoon when a head gets bonked with stars. "Boing boing."

And Stick laughs and laughs like when it's really funny and he starts to walk around and his head rolls because it is so funny and his eyes are tearing but not tears like he is sad. They look like the same tears but they aren't when you laugh and they come from a different place like they drip out from your throat and through your eyes. Tears when you are sad drip up from your heart. Stick has laughing tears and they squeeze out of his eyes and down his face. I bum-waggle again and again.

"Boing boing." I fall down and roll around in the sand.

That makes Stick laugh so hard that he can't stand up anymore and he falls down and says "Bong" in the sand. I roll and so he rolls too and we are getting sand on our skin because it is a bit wet and it sticks. I stand up and I am the sand monster.

"Roar!"

Stick takes a big clump and smacks it on his belly. It sticks there too even though the belly is so round and white. I try again and smack more on my leg. We start to smack more and more and we look like real monsters now. Stick starts to pile the sand on his hair and I rub some on his head too. I keep smooshing sand and get some from a pile that is more like mud. His hair isn't yellow anymore and his skin isn't white. He looks like a real-life sand monster and I can only tell it is still him because his eyes still poke out from all the sand. And I start getting it on my head too because that part looks cool and Jessica would think so too but she isn't here. We keep piling sand and mud on our bodies and then smacking it on each other and it might be bad or it might be good. We get to keep doing it and get as dirty as we want and it is so fun to pile sand all over and I keep doing more and more and more but no one tells us to stop. I wish Jessica was here. We play so many times.

Jessica has eight Barbies and they live in her room. I have no Barbies and I cried about it and so Momma said we could go to see Jessica's at her house one day. At Jessica's house there is one man Barbie. His name is Ken. Jessica says he counts as nine but I say no because he has a beard that you can stick on his face and take off. Ken has shorts like Jessica's dad Steven. I really like Barbies.

I asked Momma for a Barbie and she said no. I cried and stomped my leg and she still said no because Barbie only has lumps for boobs and they are too big for her waist. I cried for a whole week and even Grandpa came for dinner to help me feel better. He had a piece of lettuce in his hand. I thought Grandpa's skin was nice and thick like the lettuce except not green. Momma told Grandpa that she wouldn't buy me a Barbie. Momma said she didn't like Barbie because she didn't have a good job. Grandpa laughed. But then the next day Momma said all the Barbie talk made her feel bad and she said Jessica has lots so we can just go to her house. And we went all the time to Jessica's so I could play with them and it was really special and nice. Jessica and I got to shut the door of her room and make it into Barbie land and we built a castle and made wings and a wand and played and played. I want to go to Jessica's house now.

Between my fingers is itchy. I go to the edge of the water so I bend down to swish my hand in the water and I can see my skin again. Stick does it too because he never stops copying. There is a lot of sand on the ground even though we took so much for our bodies. I take my arm and move the sand from the skinny part of the water to outside the water. It stays in a big pile and Stick sees that it's a good idea. We both take our hands and pull sand up until we have a huge pile of it. I am the boss because I am better at sand castles so I tell Stick what to do and mostly he does. We make it like a volcano and pat the top into a point. The volcano needs a place for lava so I stick my hand in the top and Stick gets mad because he thinks I am busting it down and wants to be the one who busts. He is about to jump on the volcano but I stop him and show him how the lava will come out. He stands by and waits. I build it perfectly at the top so there is a hole for the lava that is smooth down the sides and there is a path at the top for the scientists to walk around and look in and nearly die if the volcano explodes. I need a small stick to be the scientist and he will have a dog so I need that too.

I tell Stick to look for small sticks to be on the top of the volcano. He is bad at finding sticks in the sand. He doesn't find them. He needs to get me to look and put them in his hand and he gets all happy and yells "I found it!" and holds it up like he is the king. He didn't find it and he doesn't care when I tell him again. And then I am getting tired of watching Stick and doing sand castles and of finding sticks and Stick. I am bored I don't know what we should do.

And then I am getting more tired of watching Stick because he tries to put sand in his mouth like it is lunch. I tell him no and I don't know what we should do even more and why Momma and Daddy are taking too long. We work on training Stick's inside dog like we practice all summer. I say sit and he sits. I say paw and he gives me a paw and does a really good job because he puts his tongue outside of his mouth and lets it hang down and even a little bit of spit drips from his tongue. I need a leash and a piece of grass is long enough but it is hard to tie around the dog's neck and my fingers won't. Stick won't stay still for long enough.

"Sit, Stick!"

He gets up and runs with his fat legs away.

"No." I need to punish him. I catch him and push hard. He falls back into the sand and his mouth is like an O.

I say "No! Bad dog."

Sticky cries for a minute again but then I don't care because maybe he is so bad and he makes all the bad things happen not me. When I don't care if he cries Stick usually stops so he stops. He goes onto all fours and squeals and hangs his head.

"Okay, doggie. Bad doggie," I say. I decide that Stick can be a good dog if he does tricks. I tell him this very loud and slow so he can understand. He sits and I bury his legs but he wiggles so I can't get everything covered at once. He stands up and shakes off the sand and starts to pee. I watch the pee go over and into the lake in a part circle like a rainbow.

I put my hand on my head and shake it around and dust comes out. I am very dusty everywhere and some of the dust is in my eyes. Stick dusts his hair too and it goes in his eyes and he squeezes them shut and can't see. He is stuck with his eyes shut so I have to dust the dust from his dusty eyes. But my hand has dust. My feet that are in the water aren't dusty and that's why I have to wash my hands after the bathroom so I try and get him to stick his face in the water and wash his hands. He does only a little so I start to splash him and it's funny because he is running around and screaming.

"No splash, Nana." He shakes a finger at me like a teacher and runs out of the water.

I follow him out because some of the dust is gone. Stick's hair looks gray like an old man. His body is streaked with dust and some mud and it makes him look like a zebra and he likes that because he has a book with a zebra. He neighs because he thinks it is actually a horse with stripes and maybe it is I don't know. He goes up to neigh and eat some grass. I don't care where he goes because I am tired of watching. I am too hot.

12.

I am getting mad at Momma because it is too long. I don't know why it is so long and she said "I will be there." And then this is where we are. When I get lost I am supposed to go to the meeting place that is at the front of the grocery store but there are no cash registers with many buttons or rubber belts that slide groceries here. I have worry that I am in the wrong place and maybe Momma is waiting and getting mad.

The sun is following me. I walk along the water a little and it comes right by my shoulder. I turn and walk the other way because maybe Momma is here and I don't see her. The sun is shining too much in my eyes and it walks with me. It is like a balloon that is tied onto my wrist with a string in a double knot. I don't want the balloon but there is no string so I can't let it go. It follows me no matter what I do. I walk faster and I jog and then I run and my feet go smack smack smack in the shallow water and then I stop. Sometimes I do that and Jessica will keep running right past me for tag. When I look up the sun knows that I stop and it stops too. The sun is sneakier than Jessica.

I stand for a minute and I look over and there is Gwen! She is waiting for me on a rock. I reach her and sniff and she is a little bit crunchy like cereal got on her sleeves but I love her so much. Sniffs and hugs for Gwen and we cuddle. She gets some dust on her fur but she doesn't mind and it's so good to see her. There are also my pj's and I think that they might feel good because it's like going to bed. That's what Momma said to be in a safe place and wait for her and my bed is the safest place so I'll get ready. Except we are camping so maybe my safe place is the tent or maybe the cottage or Toronto. I don't know which bed. I pick up my pj bottoms and they are a little bit almost stuck to the rock and straight and not bendy soft. The ducks have wrinkles. I hold them out to stick a foot in and they get more bendy when I wiggle them so I crunch them into a ball and they are better. I put them on and the dust is itchy but it is okay. I have to pee and I pull them down again and nearly pee in them but I don't because I bend my knees and pee in the sand just in time. I put the top on too and my skin feels a little bit sore in the dust. I sniff Gwen and look and there is Stick's pj top too. I pick it up and something is missing. I look at my legs and Stick's pants aren't here. I put them on the rock but I think Stick must have put them on already even though I didn't know he could do it.

"Sticky?"

I stand up on the rock and look around. I don't see Sticky. I hold Gwen up so she can look but she doesn't see either. I have so much worry and my stomach goes boing. I am supposed to watch Stick. But I am not a babysitter and even when I'm not watching Stick Momma felt bad for leaving too long. Jessica and

I had the castle and Ken was the bad guy trying to steal Fairy Barbie's wand and the Barbies won against him. Jessica said I was Ken the first time and so I was. And then another stealing was about to happen and she said I had to be Ken again. I said no. And Jessica said they are her Barbies so she gets to say. She said bring my own Barbies and I don't have any. Even though Momma said I could play as long as I want I was so so mad. I stomped my leg at Jessica and I went out of her room and she shut the door behind me so I was out of Barbie land then it was only Jessica's house and me.

Jessica's house is big because her mom is important and there are many rooms and I couldn't remember which. I only see Jessica's mom sometimes at the play school when we sang a song. She had black hair that had very many shines and she nodded her hair when she listened to the song and the light went twinkle. My momma's hair doesn't have as many shines and she says that is because it was yellow like Stick's and now it comes out of a bottle. I looked in Momma's room and I never see a bottle that has her hair inside. I don't know if Jessica's mom keeps her hair in bottles and maybe she has a bottle with shines in it. I wanted shines.

I went to the room that is Jessica's mom's and I think so but I'm not sure. The door is closed and I didn't know if I was bad or if the room has a bottle so I was very quiet and I sneaky turned the doorknob so I wouldn't get caught. Shines aren't for kids maybe or I won't know if babysitters can have them but I am probably not allowed until I am a grown-up. There are no shines and I can't find Momma. But then she is there anyway. She gives me a cookie and we got in the car and she says she felt bad for leaving me so long. I say give me a Barbie if you feel bad and she says no and I cry and cry so much. Daddy comes home and Momma says I didn't get a Barbie. That means that Jessica can do whatever she wants. I have to be Ken.

And the sun is hot and I close my eyes and I don't know where anyone in my family is and there is supposed to be four people and Gwen. My brain sees Stick's little round face and a smile with two dots in his cheeks and he is so sneaky and then I think oh no maybe Momma and Daddy came and got Stick. He is having snack and his belly full and his head on Momma's lap and with a cookie and I don't have it and I feel mad. I got my pj's on all by myself and had to watch Stick forever. He gets lunch and a cuddle and that is not fair. Stick didn't even put all his pj's on his body and he doesn't get my cookie. Gwen is mad too because she knows Stick always gets the special things.

"Momma?" I call out and look.

I don't see them on the lake so they must have got out of the canoe. I look up and down and I can't remember the way I ran from the sun and I'm not sure which way Momma would be.

I walk along with my feet in the water and Momma said she wouldn't leave me so long so I call out.

"Momma! Momma. I'm here. I want lunch too. Don't forget about me."

She doesn't answer and neither does Daddy and no Stick so I cry and wait. They don't come and it must be because they are so mad this time. I cry harder to show they better come soon and my tears are dropping in the water at my feet so it is getting deeper and I will drowned in the water if they don't come and get me soon. I am crying and there is a lake in my body that all the tears come from and it is getting smaller and the lake at my feet is getting bigger at the same time so my inside lake will be dry and I will die and it will be Momma's fault because she let me keep crying all day and it feels like a long time. I stop because I can't make any more tears come out. I look up and down and sniff. I can't see Momma anywhere. I wish the sun would quit following me all the time.

13.

I sing a song and walk and da da da down by the bay, where the watermelons grow and I wish I had a big piece of watermelon and I look and there is a lake and no watermelon. I am not supposed to touch the watermelon knife. They are mean to leave me with no lunch and I walk because I will show them and look over and Stick's pj top is still sitting on a rock. I think maybe Stick is still getting the cookies and he didn't get his pj's on yet and it is really really not fair. I grab the pj top because I want to show Momma that he is so naughty and she can't say it is just because he is a baby because he is not a baby. Babies can't walk and he can.

Maybe I can see the picnic blanket and I put my hands on my hips with Gwen in one and the pj top in the other and I look around and in the grass is a big round head. Sticky is there and his face is back to squished tomato and crying. He can see the pj top and knows that he is caught.

"Stick," I say.

He doesn't answer me he is crying.

"Stick?"

"Momma," he says.

"Where's Momma?" I ask.

"Momma."

And he won't give me another answer so I walk over and then I think maybe he has an owey. He looks a little bit red but not blood red just skin red. He looks sad and he is dusty and dirty and naked and I see a pile of poo is beside him. He always always poops.

I look around and he is not with Momma or Daddy and there is no lunch. I am glad that Stick didn't get lunch and I didn't either but then I feel sad because I am hungry and I wish Stick wouldn't cry.

"Hungry, Nana?" he asks.

Why does he ask me instead of Momma? I don't know where Momma is. Momma is the lunch.

"No lunch." I shake my head.

Stick is playing with a stick but I can't because there is a big hole in my tummy like if I could bend down and look then I could see right through it. I put my hand there and it still feels like my tummy but inside is the hole because it is empty. And it goes grrrr and then sounds like the washing machine when it is making the soapsuds up. Stick hears my grrrr too.

"Hungry, Nana," he says.

"I know. Me too."

"Snock?"

I know that is Stick talk for snack. "I don't have any."

"Please?"

Stick looks at me with beggy eyes but that doesn't make lunch come any more. He thinks I am his babysitter again and that my counter has bread and butter and bananas and maybe even jam. Or pancakes with lots of syrup would be best and some bacon that is soft not burned. I can smell bacon in the air and I look around because I think that someone is cooking it and not sharing and being sneaky but I don't see anyone at all. It is empty all around us the trees on one side and the wet and mushy grass on the other.

"Hungry," says Stick.

Momma is gone so so long. I have worry that I am in trouble because I don't listen. I think what Momma said that she will be there. I am supposed to wait in a safe spot and I think that is my bed. Except we are not in Toronto and not at the cottage so then I sleep in the tent. I don't know anything. I stand up and go to where the water licks the corner of my toes and look at the water. Across the lake is a land and maybe the tent is there and I can take Stick for a ride and go. I have to squint my eyes because there are jewels on the water except not really diamonds just twinkles from the sun. On the land across I see something move and it is in the bushes. It is on the other side of the water away but I can see.

I watch and I see something moving in the trees on that land. It is a black thing and my tummy knows it's the black dog. I feel scared and glad to be on this land. The black dog is moving on the land and is sniffing. The air comes out of me in huffs. I hold my breath make it stop and I see that the black dog is nosing around and sniffing and walking to the water that is across the lake from me. I stay quiet and try not to breathe and hope Stick will stay quiet too. The black dog is nosing around like Snoopy but more like the raccoon. Snoopy would be looking for Mrs. Buchanan to get in trouble or even Momma. He wouldn't be just nosing around like there was no trouble. The black dog is more like the raccoon and sniffs and eats something and puts his nose in the air. He sticks his nose out and sniffs for a minute and then walks slowly along the water.

I know that dogs can swim because I have seen Snoopy swim. He came up to our cottage and he was in the water and there was another summer friend dog named Fergus. He is short and fat. His hair is white and I tried to take him in for a swim and his momma said no. Fergus hates water same as Stick. Fergus fell in when he was getting out from a boat and the water was bad ever since. So Snoopy was at my cottage and jumped off the dock into the air after a ball and Fergus just got to watch and wag wag wag. I get worried that the black dog will jump into the lake and is coming for us but he stops. His toes at the water like mine. Both our toes are inside the lake and I can feel that he knows and I know it is like we are touching across the water. He keeps his nose sniffing up in the air. I can see him more now because he is out from the bushes and his fur is very black. His belly is big and his legs are short. I let go of my breath and feel phew.

He is a black dog that isn't a swimming dog. He is more like a bear than a swimming dog, except he isn't brown like Gwen or a real bear. If I threw a ball into the water he would not jump off a dock just wag wag wag. My family isn't scared of bears. They come around the cottage to remind Daddy that he didn't scrub the barbecue enough and left a piece of hot dog that was burned on there so I didn't want to eat it and I make Daddy cut it off. Momma said that was very bad because then we get the bears used to us so we never do that anymore. If I don't like a burned hot dog I gave it to Stick. And sometimes he won't eat it so I peel off the skin of the hot dog because they look like a finger but really they are more like trees and you can take off the burned bark and the inside is fine. Stick will eat it. Then when Momma asks if I ate it I can say yes and get a cookie. When our family sees a bear I never saw it. Daddy is the only one who got to. We just stay away and sometimes we make noise with two pots that we bang together. Momma says to tell the bear "Yo, bear" but I never say "Yo, dog" so I don't say anything. I listen to see if Momma is banging a pot and she isn't. I don't hear any pots and no one yelling. The black dog has a big nose and it just sniffs the air and I don't have to be scared because of water. But I have to be careful of strange dogs.

I watch the black dog and I feel like it is watching me with the tip of its nose. I watch like on TV when animals are inside there. I wonder if Momma can see it or if she is still asleep or she might be gone away. I know that if there are no pots she is not near it. The black dog noses around and it grabs something in its mouth and I look and I can't tell what it is besides long. But it waves around and on the end it's red and it might be the meat with Daddy's sneaker. Daddy won't like a bear chewing his sneaker.

"Hey," I say.

The black dog looks up for a minute and sniffs like I don't matter. I watch and he goes back to the meat and he sits on the ground and chews his bone. I put my hands on my belly and it feels weird.

I hear Stick making noises behind me.

"I pooed," he says and with crying eyes.

I look and he is sitting with a naked bum and there is still the pile of poo beside him and yuck. It's like he thinks I am his momma and do poo and lunches now and I don't like it no thanks. I don't help him. I wrinkle my nose and lift Gwen for a sniff.

"Hi, Glen," he says.

That is nice and I sniff her. Gwen feels like we share with her. My momma says it can be hard with only three people but Stick and Gwen and I are used to each other. I stick Gwen out to kiss Stick on the cheek because she is quite kissy and that's what she wants to do. Stick's tears have stopped and he even smiles and I see the two dimples that are like when a stick goes in the marshmallow and a hole is left in it.

"Sanks, Glen," says Stick to Gwen.

"Are you okay?" I ask.

Stick stands up on his fat legs and shows me his pooey bum. Yuck.

"Bitchy," he says.

He is itchy. He means I have to watch him more. Things like diapers mean you are a babysitter but I am not. I take a breath out my nose and it makes me sound like Momma when I do that. I do it again because when the air is coming out my nose I can't smell the poo and that is better. I do it again and again but then my head feels like the balloon would pop so I stop. It floats back into my nose and smells like the time Daddy forgot and left the diaper in the car and we drove around with the poo by accident. Gwen says she will help me and I think I will help Stick because we are three.

I put Gwen and Stick's pj top in one hand and take Stick's hand like a babysitter even though I am not. We step carefully up the hill with grass to get away from his poo. We have to climb up and that is okay because sometimes Stick sits in the dirt and that will be a bit less for me to fix. We get to the top and I look and I see there is a forest here and a slide down to more grass. I tell Stick to lie down like when he gets diapers at night and I don't have wipes or a washcloth like Momma. There is a green leaf and a few more on a plant and I take it and wipe and it smells like it tastes like a sour candy that makes my two sides of my cheeks get pulled into my mouth. There isn't that much, so it is actually pretty easy and Gwen and I are good moms. Stick stands up and I make him put his pj top on. He wants the pants but I don't know about those. He stamps his leg but that doesn't make the pants come back. His little dingle just wiggles.

"Juice," says Stick.

Me too. And Gwen. We are still always thirsty. I stand up and look down and see if we walk along the side of the trees they open up to a grassy spot and there is a little water trickling down. I say pretend it is juice and apple or orange and take Stick's and Gwen's hands and we walk over and there is a little pool of water like chocolate milk. I kneel down and put my lips in it and suck in like a straw except I don't have one. I get mud in my teeth and I sit up and chew and it crunches. Stick laughs and he wants chocolate milk and puts his head down to the pool and I think about how a bad girl would smoosh his head in the water and I don't because I am the one watching. He lifts up his face again and says he can't get any into his mouth.

I tell Stick it's like a straw and he has to suck in and we both make sucking noises for a minute and it is funny and then he tries to drink again and I put my knees down and this time I know it is wet ground and a little like a sponge which is funny because Stick is on the sponge except in no pj bottoms so only me is getting wet at the knees. But not that wet and Gwen is dry because I hold her up. Stick isn't getting water through his no straw so he starts licking the water like Snoopy. That is funny too and I laugh and he laughs and then he can't lick and laugh so he tries to smoosh his cheeks back down so he can drink. He tips forward a little and gets his face wet and might cry but I say it is funny so he laughs.

"Juice," he says again.

I put Gwen between my legs to hold and I scoop my hand in the chocolate milk water so I am holding it. Stick puts his face in my hand and he gets drinking like that. I put two hands together and scoop and it gets more in his lips. I do it again and I look at the water and see little pieces of dirt but they look like nice dirt not bad. Stick drinks all that and so I get a bit more and this time a fish! It is small and clear and has legs sort of like a crab but sort of like a spider and maybe not a fish but something crawly. Stick puts his face in to drink it.

"No, Stick. There's a fish."

"Where?" He looks behind him.

"There!" I point down but my fingers can't point because they are making the bowl that holds the fish like a fish tank.

"Where?" He looks down into the muddy water in the pool.

Finally I put my hands up near his face so his eyes can't look anywhere else and he sees it.

"Fishie!"

He is excited too and we watch it scratch at my hands except I can't feel it but a small tickle.

We are busy watching the fish and I see something moving out of the corner of my eye but I don't care because the fish is trying to crawl out the side. It looks not happy to be in my hands or like it is worried and I think about squeezing my hand to crush it. I close my fingers but Stick makes me open them again because he wants to see. But I am the boss of it and the fish can't get away and I don't care about Stick so I smack my hands together and squish squish roar.

"Hey," says Stick.

"I must crush you," I say in my deepest voice and I am a pretend big man with muscles like Daddy's. I open my hands again and look. There is no fish and the water has fallen back into the puddle and we look but no fish. It must be scared of me and it ran away. Or it fell back in the puddle or I crushed its body so we can't see it anymore.

"Here, fishie fishie." Stick is looking around the ground.

The corner of my eye sees something again. It is brown and over in the part where there are no trees and more grass. It has fur and it moves and that makes me turn my head. It is half in the grass and an animal. I think oh neat because I like animals and especially tigers. This is not a tiger because there are not orange and black stripes. The fur is brown and the body is big and it is like a blob sitting in the grass. I think it is cute for a second and maybe a hippo like at the zoo and then it moves a big head around to look at us and I feel a little scared. There is no fence and it is not that far away. And you have to be careful about animals I remember. Even Snoopy. They don't speak English and can get confused like Stick except that he is human too. No fur. This animal doesn't look mad but I don't know if he likes us or not. He starts to move and I put a hand down to grab Gwen and sniff. The animal steps up onto a harder part in the dirt and I see it is huge and it has four legs that used to be in the water and now they aren't.

"Look, Stick," I whisper. "A horsie."

Stick looks over and his mouth goes into an O and he is quiet. He turns to me and puts his pointy finger to his lips and says "Shh." He is squatting down and has his hands on his knees. This is funny because when we are at the zoo he always shouts at the animals and Daddy says no. We are not supposed to shout or bang the glass because it gives the animals headaches and they have to put up with a lot. I watch it too and it is standing now up higher so I can see that it has legs that are really long. Now he is standing on them. It has a smooth fur that is brown and darker than Gwen. I think it is probably a horse with big lips because of the eyes at the side of its head. A horse can see backwards to run from people if it needs to. And big ears that might make it a donkey but it does not make donkey noises. It got a haircut because it has bangs that are straight across and not in his eyes. That is like how the lady cuts my bangs and sometimes I wish they could stay long but then I can't see where I am going. The horse doesn't make any noises. It just stands and looks at us and chews.

"Moose," says Stick.

The horse blinks and chews some more.

"It's a horsie."

"No."

I feel fed up having to talk to babies. "A moose has big antlers on its head like a coatrack."

"Moose."

I think of our book of animals and we read it with Daddy and there are girl mooses and they maybe look like that with no antlers but Stick is too much of a baby to be right. "Horse."

"Moose," he whispers and I should give him a smack but I

don't care. I just don't want to only play with him and it would be good if Jessica was here. But we keep watching the horse and it eats some grass and then turns and walks off the other way and we can't see it anymore. I feel like when we went to the zoo except no McDonald's. I am so hungry.

14.

Also there is more windy and I feel a little colder on my legs. It is going to be nighttime and we need to get to our safe place. I pull on Stick's arm so he will stand up and come because I think no more water on my legs it's too cold so we walk over to the trees part. It is darker because the trees are spread out like a roof all over the top. Our safe place can be at the cottage because we have two beds. Or Toronto and we need to find it. We walk in there for a little bit and the feet don't hurt until a pine needle decides to prick them ouch. Mostly they don't prick only a few mean ones. Stick gets them too because he says "Owey" and stops and makes me look at his foot.

"Gotta splinter."

He is scared of splinters because he got one and Momma and I had to go to the summer friends' house to have them help us hold him down so Momma could take it out with pointers. Stick said "No, don't touch" but Momma said yes because the splinter could get sick and die in his foot and then the dead body would make him sick. Finally she got it out with the pointers and showed us in a lamp and I looked and it was a small piece of the dock. So the splinter body was on the dock at first and so watch out when you walk there. Maybe wear shoes so no bodies go in your feet. And so Stick thinks there are bodies around the needles and I try to look at his foot and he holds it up but he falls. He almost cries but I tell him he is okay and I don't know but no blood. Because I am the big sister and I say he is okay he is okay and doesn't cry. When he is sitting on the ground I can look at where he got the splinter before. But he won't keep his foot still and pulls it back and he doesn't want me to look or pull his feet away all the time. I say to him to stay still but he is making the sad noise of his inside dog. I feel bad. I put the inside dog there. I made it stay.

"Do you want Gwen?" I ask.

He nods. It is very Stick to talk with his head instead of his mouth.

"Here," I say and hand him Gwen.

"Glen." He cuddles her and I think maybe it was a mistake because he will get used to her and love her so much that he thinks he loves her more than me. So I grab his foot to keep him from going away.

Stick is scared when I grab his foot because it makes him think splinter.

"Hug Gwen and sniff and don't look," I tell him.

He cuddles her to his face and closes his eyes. "Okey."

I take his foot and I look at the same spot and see that there is no splinter so it is okay and no blood or body at all.

"You're fine, Stick. Don't worry," I say.

He nods and sniffs Gwen again. "Glen."

"You are brave," I say because that's what Momma would say. He does another sniff.

"Can I have her back now?" I stick out my hand.

He sticks out a fat arm and gives her. I feel really glad and sniff and she stinks a little like Stick but not too bad.

"Good dog," I say to him. "Good, good dog."

"Woof!" He keeps his bum on the ground but puts his arms up in the air and shuffles his feet around in the needles. His face looks pleased and I think he knows that he is older and growing up from not a baby. He can be brave with splinters now.

But then splinters are whatever because I am so hungry and Momma has not come like she said. I look from there and close by I can see a bunch of dangle berries. They are hiding under leaves so sneaky. I couldn't see them from walking but down here on the needles I can see where they are. I keep on my hands and knees so they don't run and sneak up. Grrrr I growl at them because my stomach does too and when lions are going to eat deers they don't roar so then I think be quiet and sneak. The dangle berries don't see me and I put one paw in front of the other and sneak up and then pounce. I get the plant under my paw and reach down and pick off a berry with my teeth. And then I stop and the dangle berry is in my mouth and I worry that it is red and might be the spicy kind of red. I take it out of my mouth with my fingers and look and sniff. It has a red stem in one end and a skinny brown stem on the other side and it is red but not like a cherry more like an apple except really small like a blueberry but it isn't any of these. I stick my tooth in and a little juice comes out and I lick and it is spicy like the gum my momma chews not like hot but I like bubble gum better. I bite and it is a little bit like a mint spicy and not bad and I have another. And there is a plant beside so I pluck those and stick them in my mouth. I find another plant and then I hear breathing behind me.

"Hey, want some." Stick has words in his head and they come out more when he is hungry.

I don't want to share. I want to eat everything because the hole in my tummy is so big I need to plug it. I push Stick back and eat another berry and then the breathing again and I look and he has big sad eyes like his inside dog and they make my stomach sag.

"Okay, one." I pass him one.

He gobbles it up like it is a cookie and it isn't and I wish we still had those and where is the tin? But I don't care because I am picking the berries off and shoving them in my mouth and the hole is big so I need lots.

"More," he says.

Huff.

"More, Nana." His small paw wipes my back.

"Here." I show him a plant and shrug. "Take some if you want it."

He smiles this big smile like I just gave him a candy but I didn't it's healthy for my body and Momma would say that's good so I should tell her when she comes to get us that it was good food I made for lunch and not junk. Stick puts his fat finger on the berry and pulls it down and it won't come off. I try not to look because I need to eat many many berries and it doesn't feel like there is another and his hand is there again and pulls and the berry falls off and rolls down into the dirt.

"Hey," says Stick like the plant is playing a trick on him.

"Here." I pick the berry off the ground and give it to him and then I keep plucking and eating some more and too many are getting spicy but at least it is good spice. Stick tries to get more with his useless fat hands but they don't work. My momma said they didn't work at all when he was a first-born baby but I remember him holding Arrowroot cookies so that was probably wrong. He didn't have teeth but he smooshed the Arrowroot on his gums for so long that enough spit went in and it made the cookie mushy and so he kind of drank it but was kind of chewing it with his gums too but not teeth.

"Help," he says.

I give him one more. "That's all."

"Please?"

"No. All done."

"Okey," he says and he sounds sad in his throat.

I feel sadder because I am so hungry but looking at him feels like there is a beanbag in my chest. Like we have to run around in the school at gym time and pick up for a relay and it flops over and is dirty on the other side from so many grubby hands. Huff.

I tell him to sit and I take a leaf and fold it around another leaf and that is his bowl. I tell him to sit and stay and put Gwen down to sit in his lap because she needs someone to hold her and I need both my hands so at least Stick is a good Gwen holder because he gives her back. I find the next plant and I scrape the berries into my hand and I pour half but maybe just less but I am bigger into Stick's bowl and I shove the others into my mouth. I move over to pick more.

"Gums," he says.

I pour more into his bowl. Minty gum that he sneaks from

Momma's purse and is not allowed and he swallows it and it's the sort of thing that might make Daddy go away. Stick pushes the berries into his mouth and is breathing through his nose because his mouth is closed and busy chewing and he makes whuffle noises and that means it is really good and I am doing a good job. I go to the plant place again and get more and dump them in mouth and bowl and he keeps chewing and I give him more. He is chewing and then he takes one berry and I am about to tell him not to throw them because none should go on the ground they should go into my mouth. He doesn't throw it but he pinches his between his thumb and fat finger and then holds it to Gwen's mouth. She doesn't eat it because she only has black string and no mouth but he doesn't know because he makes a smacking sound for her to eat and asks her if it is yummy. Gwen looks happy and I can see her heart is chewing even if her mouth stays still.

I keep getting berries until I have to walk farther away and then I go back and forth and then a plant is closer to the wet grass and then there are no more plants with the dangle berries and they are gone. I walk back across the line that I plucked and I find a couple and I come back and sit down beside Stick and Gwen and I eat three and I give Stick three and we chew and they are gone. We are both not talking and picking in our mouths for anything left.

"Thank you, Nana."

"Yeah."

And I am not just watching I am like a babysitter and I'm too young and I didn't listen to Momma. We sit beside each other and stare at the trees and I think of hot dogs and wonder if I can smell bacon except I can't because we are alone.

15.

The trees that we are in make it dark but also the sky turns night. The sun is peeking through the trees at the side and it looks at us and we sit and we don't know what to do and the sun just stays but then it starts to go away more. I watch it and I can see the bottom part is behind some trees. Stick plays with a rock like it is a ball and I can't see the sun move but more of it goes until it is only half a sun. We sat on the dock at my cottage and watched it across the lake one day and it was after a storm. We had no lights and my momma had candles out and ready and she gave Stick and me flashlights so we don't need to be scared and we took blankets to sit on the dock and watch the sun go to bed. When it was tucked in we went back up and the cottage was gray until it turned black. My momma said don't be scared because it is the same earth just not as light.

I said I wanted to kiss Daddy good night and Momma said he isn't at the cottage and that he is not coming up. I knew he would come on the weekend and Momma said no and Daddy is not in our family he is in Toronto. She put her hand on her mouth and said "Oh, sweetie." I saw a little piece of sad drip from her heart up into her eyes but she didn't show me her cry and I didn't see it because she swallowed it back into her heart. Our house is in Toronto and we are four. At the cottage we were three.

We made a fort with all the pillows in the middle of the floor by the couch and Momma put two chairs on the other side and blankets were over the top for the roof. We all cuddled inside. Momma said it needed a name and I said it was Fort Anna and Momma said it had to be a better name for all of us. Momma said we should call it Fort Whyte because it had nearly our whole family. It got dark and Momma sings and Stick is asleep and snores in like three seconds because he always falls asleep really fast. I listened to Momma's song and I was awake and she stopped singing and I wasn't scared. I woke up in the morning and gave Gwen a sniff and it was my bed around me. I could see the swirly part of the knots of the wood that is on the wall in my cottage. The light beside my bed was on. Stick was breathing in the bed beside mine that is his bed and he was on his tummy with his bum up in the air.

Fort Whyte stayed up. My momma came out of her room and soon Daddy's room and she rubbed her eyes and her hair is mussy in the back with a black bendy that bunches up from her pillow. She had Daddy's boxer underpants on because there is a place for a penis even though Daddy doesn't use it. Momma only wears man's underpants when she misses Daddy and maybe his T-shirt too. She looked at me and smiled and told me to come here with only her hand. We crawled into Fort Whyte and we got under the sleeping bag because it was still cold. She put her arms around me and it was the warmest place to be. I said I love the fort and she said that she knows and that it can stay.

Stick and I sit. The sun has just a little tip that I can still see and I know that soon it will go gray and it is black after that. I stand up and look around and Stick looks at me.

"Don't leave, Nana."

"I'm not. I'm looking."

Stick stands up and stands right behind me. I feel hot on my face because there is no fort and no sleeping bag and not even a tent and I don't want to be in trees. My bones are made of rock on the inside and I need to make a lot of muscle just to pick up one foot. I take a few steps and am looking around and Stick's nose is breathing right behind me and it's a little bit chilly. I turn and look at him and even no pants. But he is fat and his bones don't rattle like mine because he is more fatter. The only thing I see that is like our fort is a tree that tipped over. The bottom sticks up like a hand spread out and the tree lies on the ground except for a little fort that is not a castle but it would be if it had a tall tower and gold and is right where the tree stuck into the ground before it tipped. I tell Stick to come and we walk over and I can see that there is a little part that has a roof that could be over us a little bit.

"There, Stick." I point. "That's bed."

"Bed?"

"Like a fort."

"Fort?" He sounds excited and looks around for our couch and there is no couch.

"Not Momma's fort. Our fort."

Stick looks at the dark spot under the tree. "Momma's fort."

"Not a castle because no tower."

"Momma?"

"Momma's not here."

His lip sticks out and I can tell he feels scared and I don't really like the fort so much because it will never be as good as Momma's.

I get on my hands and knees and crawl under the tree. There are pine needles all on the ground and those are the bottom of the bed and that is dry. The tree is higher up at the start and then gets lower down when the tree goes to the ground so I can put my head and shoulders at the higher part and it slips down to just past my feet if I curl my knees a little bit. I turn on my back and look up and the tree looks like flaky skin but a spicier smell that I like not gum. I turn over to look the other way and it is open and I can see trees and they are darker gray now.

I wish our fort was more like a castle and maybe sides like the blanket made so you could see out between the chairs and that was the door. I leave Gwen inside because she is very tired and wants to sleep and I crawl back out and see Stick's dingle is peeing on the ground and I walk around the end of the tree. There are branches on the ground from the tree and two have broken off but they still have the needles on. I pull these up and balance them on the tree and it is hard and I can only get one because it hogs the space and I can't get the other one up without knocking everyone off so I just do one. I go back around and look in and it is see-through in the back like the air is sticking through the needles but the blanket had little holes too and it is okay. Stick squats down with his hands on his knees and his dingle pointing out and it is darker gray now and he looks in but he maybe can't see me. Everything around us is more grayer and grayer and soon we won't see so much and I feel shaky like cold and nervous in my belly.

Stick is waiting. "Bedtime?"

"I don't know."

He moves his head to the side like he doesn't understand because he doesn't and I don't too.

"Come inside, Stick," I say.

"Nana?"

"Yes." I pick Gwen up to snuggle.

Stick just does a few loud nose breaths and doesn't say.

"Go to sleep, Sticky."

"Bedtime?"

My knee goes in Stick's pee and I think huff and I lie on my side and it feels better with something at the back of the fort. I close my eyes and put my hands out and make a wish for a blanket and a flashlight and maybe I am asking so I will also need Momma and a cookie that I eat not decorate and Daddy too. I open my eyes and no. Just Stick. We are two.

16.

My head feels fuzzy like my tongue and I can't think what I am doing lying under a tree and it is dark and we aren't supposed to be in the forest with no Momma or Daddy and this far from the cottage except when we go in the canoe and then the tent is like the cottage and not too far from that but it is not here. Stick is like the fire. But just warm not so hot for cooking marshmallows so Gwen and I snuggle into him. He fits against my chest and his little bum is against my legs so I hope that he doesn't pee. More important he is warm. I wish I was allowed a marshmallow. I put my arm around him so Gwen is near my shoulder and Sticky is like a big Gwen. His big clunky head is rattling around and he puts it on my arm to rest like a pillow. I wish I had one. He stops wiggling and it is a little bit warmer. Best would be a blanket and more food and really big marshmallows that were as big as Stick's head so it would take all night to eat. I could eat the middle and then curl up inside it and be so so cozy. I think do princesses sleep in marshmallow and they probably do.

I hear eeeeeee and I hate that sound. It is by my ear and I can't see but I know because I've gotten lots of bites before that it is a mosquito. They like my blood a lot. I use my hand to thump and I try to smoosh it against my ear. The eeeeeee stops and I think ha-ha! I close my eyes again and then nothing and then eeeeeee. I want to call Momma in to turn on the light and smack it. She is the best smacker in our family and can do smacks even in the dark or in a tent and she puts her finger and just goes squish on the top. It is gentle and nice like they are lucky that they got smacked by the tip of her finger only. My daddy won't use hands he uses a flyswatter because he says he doesn't want their bodies on his hand. Sometimes if they had bitten there is blood too and that is gross. I think so too so it's better when the swatter or Momma does it but now it's my hand and no light to see it. I feel it touch my cheek like a little tickly feather and I smack my face but still eeeeeee. I don't like it and I thought Momma said no more mosquitoes for the year. I remember the time my eye got a bite on the top and it got puffy so I looked like someone punched me in the face but they didn't. A mosquito stuck a straw into my skin to drink from me like a juice box. And then spit in poison like putting your spit back into the juice box. That is gross if anyone else wants a sip. The spit made my eye puff and I could almost not see except I could see pink skin that was puffy and hanging down a bit into my eyeball. When I touched it I could see my fingertips there but the skin didn't feel like mine.

I make my hand go back and forth fast by my ear because sometimes you can fan a mosquito and they can't stay on the air they mean to and go sideways instead of forward. Like if someone picked up the sidewalk I was walking on and wiggled it up and down so I fell off like by accident. I think it is going over near to Stick and it stops and everything is quiet again. I didn't smoosh it and I don't know if I fanned it away. I think it might be sticking a straw into Stick and that is better than me. He is so soft and cushy that he is probably the best juice box a mosquito can find and I bet that little fella mosquito is pretty happy and soon I hear eeeeeee. But it is slower and I picture him carrying a tiny juice box that is full of Stick's blood and he is holding with his feet and having to flap his tiny wings really hard. They are so thin they look like paper except paper that you could see through like you use to wrap a present. Eeeeeee eeeeeee and then it gets quieter eeee and a little tiny piece of time and buzz and it goes away and I can't hear it. Phew.

I curl my legs up more around Stick and his skin is cold but the bones inside are warm so I stay really close. I think he is asleep but not yet which is good because I am lonely. When he falls asleep and we share a room and it's always him falling asleep faster than me. Momma says I take longer to turn off my brain and it would be nice if I could have a switch like I use to turn off the light and just go click. That's what Stick does because the switch is on his eyelids so he closes them and click. I lift my head a little to see if he has flicked his eyeballs shut. I bang my head on the tree. I have never had a tree sticking across my bed before so I forgot it was doing that. I lift my head more slowly until it just rests on the tree and I remember the spicy that I like. I can see Stick's eyes are a little open and a little shut. He knows that I am moving and doesn't want to get left behind. He is checking on me moving but can't stay awake. I put my head back down and I won't ever sleep a long time maybe forever.

17.

My eyes open and my hand is in the needles patting them. I am scared and I don't know what is happening and then my hand touches Gwen's fur and my breath gushes out of my body. I thought she is lost but she is not. I hug her tight and sniff and I am so glad and so happy that it was not true. When you have a dream and it feels real it means you might pee the bed. I need to pee. And I shout and shout and Daddy doesn't come. He helps me pee at night if I am scared because sometimes there can be monsters in a closet or under a bed at night and you never know. It is only Stick lying here. He rolls over and boinks me with his head. His nose breath goes in and out. We are two. I don't want Stick I want Daddy and I miss him so much it makes my tummy feel weird. Daddy is warm and he tastes like salt on his arm. He has big eyebrows that go up when he is laughing and big teeth too. He has a temper and that means that you tiptoe when his eyebrows are down.

When Daddy's eyebrows are down that is a very important thing and it doesn't mean that Daddy is bad. It does mean that if I am naughty his hair will get more sticky up on his head and his big teeth show. He growls sometimes. That is not because he doesn't love me but he is tired or hungry so it's not just his belly that growls but his mouth too. We read a book that we both love that is about a boy named Charlie who loves chocolate like me. I like Veruca because she is a bit naughty. Daddy says it's what you imagine sometimes comes true. I say what does that mean? He says what you have is always better than you imagine in your head so be careful what you wish. Because it could come true and that could be the worst.

I am not in bed and there are sounds like animals outside and I feel so scared. Daddy is mad and isn't here. His face was outside the car. I was in the backseat with Stick and Gwen and Momma had her hands on the steering wheel and turning it and her face white and stone. Daddy's seat was empty because he was standing outside and I looked at him and I wanted him inside the car. His head came closer to my window and he put his hand on my glass and I saw it big and lines like roads and the one where it means you live a long life. "I love you, Anna" he said to me and the sound is foggy because of glass. I tried to hold his hand but I can only touch the window.

I thought he was pulling his hand away and I wanted to roll down the window to touch it so I tell him to put his hand back. But I saw the driveway turn. The car was going away. His hand was still in the same place and his face looked like when he ate a lemon with no cake around it. The car goes vroom. We were going to the cottage for a long time. I told Momma to stop because we were leaving Daddy. She didn't talk and doesn't look and we are going down the street. I turned and saw Daddy standing only by himself all alone. I yelled for Daddy and he got smaller and smaller until he was only like my thumb. And then he was gone away.

"Momma," I shout.

I wait for a minute and I am outside. I only see Stick. No one is there only an animal and it is so close I feel like it will come and get me. I open my eye crack and look and it is so dark. I am not in bed and the needles are pricking a part where my pj's are sagging down my bum like always. I pull them up. It is cold and no blanket to pull to my chin. The animal is making a deep growl and I wish I already went home. I open my eyes more and the animal keeps growling like he doesn't even want my eyes to open but I am too scared not to see him so I keep looking. When I can't see in the dark my momma says to keep looking and my eyes will know when they have enough time to see in the dark. And my eyes start to know and I can see the tree up close to my head. The animal must see that too and won't drag because I am in a cave so it is waiting for me to come out. I look out and it is very dark. I see the shape of a tall tree standing in the forest and there is another one. After that comes the open part where the horse was chewing.

I can't see the animal but then maybe I can. A black shape is close to the tree and it has a low growl that goes grrrr gaaaa grrrr gaaaa to let me know that it is there. And it is going to eat me because I don't have an army or sword except the one in my mind and I can't find it. Gwen is by my face and very scared because she hears and the grrrr gaaaa and we both stare out to hope that our eyes will see the animal better so we can know where to run. It has a dark color and it looks round on top like a hump and it must be very big from the sounds. I can't see the eyes and no teeth but I know from the sounds that it is show-ing teeth like Snoopy does at the mailman and Mrs. Buchanan grabs Snoopy under the jaw and they look at each other in the eyes and Mrs. Buchanan says "Oh, what did that poor man do to deserve such poor treatment from you?" And that's when I know it is the black dog.

My heart rolls out of my chest and onto the ground and I can't push it back in. I am shaking and I know I am scared but then my legs are wet and it is warm for a minute and Gwen is on my face so I reach down and it's wet and I peed. Okay because a lit-tle warmer but then it is cold right away and I am shaking so I couldn't help it. I don't know how big the black dog is and I don't know if he will drag me out from the tree. Grrrr gaaaa grrrr gaaaa it keeps going to scare me and I wish it would just bite be-cause I don't want to be so scared anymore. I wish I didn't have to be under a tree and my stomach keeps rolling in and out. The shakes make it feel like my bones are going to rattle out of my body or my knees are coming apart. I stare and the black dog is just sitting like when the lions are watching the deers and wait-ing for them to move so they can jump and rip with claws and then bite on necks and even ride on the back of the deer when it tries to run.

The black dog is waiting for me to move because that is when he knows I have seen him so I know the thing is that I can't move or let him know that I can see him sitting like a black hump. Grrrr gaaaa he makes the growl but he thinks I can't hear that because it is like breathing to him. No one thinks that any-one else can hear them breathe so I have to lie very still. Gwen and I don't move and my pee is freezing on my leg and stink but

I leave it there. My knees keep shaking and I wish I could put my hands on them to stop the top caps from coming loose but that would be moving and the black dog would know. I barely breathe I am so still because that is the only way I can stay alive. The black dog will attack if I move. So I just stay still. I don't even move my finger.

18.

There is light in my eye crack and I am so cold. I listen and grrrr gaaaa and I remember the black dog and I open my eye crack. Gwen is with me. I peek out and can't see the black dog. Only a stump with green mossy mossy and pine needles and a tree and another tree so the black dog has snuck around. Grrrr gaaaa it sounds like his breath but I look down and the sound is coming from Stick. His nose says grrrr gaaaa. He must have heard the black dog and is trying to make a sound the same or I don't know. Maybe Stick thinks that if he makes the same noise that he will scare the black dog and it will go away because it is the scariest thing on earth so it can only be scared of itself. Or he thought the black dog would drag him away and my bones are still shaking but more from cold than scared right now. Gwen is okay and Stick's big head is on my arm. I try to push on my arm to sit up but I can't. I think my arm is gone and it won't move.

That's when I know the black dog did chew it off. It is off from my shoulder.

I look at my fingers on the other side of Stick's sleepy head and they can't move. They are sausages. I try to wiggle and nothing. I reach over Stick's big head and touch the sausage fingers and they are cold and look blue and were in the fridge or the freezer and is frozen and just needs to be cooked to eat so that must be the black dog's plan.

"Sticky?" I whisper.

"Wha?" His eyes are glued shut a little and he is so dirty he should take a bath.

"My hand is eaten."

Stick sits up and looks like he is sitting on the moon. "Momma?"

"My hand died," I say and I am still on the needles because it is hard to move with a sausage on your body. I try to wiggle my fingers for him to show him that I can't wiggle my fingers but he doesn't know what I am doing because there is nothing. "I can't move it."

He looks at my hand and looks back at me. I know his eyes mean he is hungry and I am hungry too and maybe he means he wants to eat my hand if that is all he says about my hand and I hope not.

"Band-Aid?"

I know he wants one but only cuts with blood get Band-Aids or else Stick wanted to have them all over his knees just because he had a bang.

And then the needles on the ground start to prickle in my hand and ouch it hurts too much. I sit up and bang my head on the tree ouch. Stick jumps out of our bed to get out of the way and aaaaah my arm is being attacked by needles except now I am standing and the needles are not touching my arm but their needle eyes have laser beams because they are still poking everywhere in my hand. I can move it and I try to hit it with my other. I jump around but nothing makes the needles stop poking even invisible needles. It hurts so so much and Stick just watches because there is no blood or Band-Aids. I jump around and it feels a little better but my thumb is stabbed. And my fingers are curled around and now they can go straight. I can feel my own hand and I ask it to make a punching fist and it does. I keep moving it because I can't believe it was cut off and now it is back on and moving like a magic trick. I stand and look at it because I thought I would be a one-arm girl forever and ever. Stick is standing watching me and he doesn't know what is going on and all he does is let a tiny pee come out of his dingle. He is too much of a baby to tell him what happened and what I saw in the night. He would get scared and cry too much but I know. The black dog is making war.

I take Stick over to the chocolate milk water in the little pool and I drink and I use my hands to help him drink and we don't catch a fish. It is cold and we both are tired. I lead Stick back to the tree.

"We need Momma and Daddy," I say to Stick.

Stick says "Yes" but he looks very sad and tired and his face is more like a pudgy tomato today than it is normally. I touch his cheek and it is hot and leaves a finger mark that is white. I watch my finger mark and it stays there for a minute and then it fades but not back to normal skin it goes red.

"Ouch," says Stick.

I look at my arm and it is the same with a fingerprint but not as strong and that might be because it's my own finger. Not such a white mark comes. If someone else tried to make a fingerprint in me it would be whiter like happened on Stick. Except Stick's finger is too small and so it doesn't count and there is no one else.

We had fingerprints when we were at the cottage and it was too much sun. The sun was very hot and it reached down and made heat on my skin in a burn. I was supposed to wear a T-shirt when I went in the lake. A T-shirt swims around when I tried to swim and it floats out and was pulling me down into the water. I told Momma that I couldn't swim with the T-shirt and so she said we had to go inside then and got mad. That was when Stick got lost at the cottage and I think she was already mad about that too and it was going to happen soon. We were playing and Momma was making dinner and she said harrumph many times because she didn't have Daddy help. She said that I need to act bigger now and start to be a more help. I was supposed to watch Stick and play and then I said I should get Jell-O for dessert because I never got to eat it before. I found a small box that she told me is Jell-O. Jessica told me that Jell-O wiggles and it is the best. I don't know how it wiggles because I shook the box and it sounds like there is sand I think of sand like at the beach. Momma got mad because I am saying that I am not old enough to do babysitting for money. I was just supposed to play. I got mad too because I don't get Jell-O. I found it in the cupboard and want it for dinner and she says "I don't trust that stuff" and doesn't like it wiggling and thinks yuck. She really huffs and stamps off down to the bedroom and her feet are so mad they go flop flop flop in the flip-flops and she goes away. Stick has his hands on his ears and I feel sad.

I wanted Gwen and she was sitting on my cottage bed and we cuddled.

But then later Momma called "Stick, Alex, Sticky, answer me, sweetie," and Gwen and I found out that Sticky was gone. Momma was screaming at the cottage and begging Stick to come out and worried about the water and snakes and yelled and told me to yell but then she said "Don't yell—let's be quiet because he might be afraid." Gwen and I whispered "Here, Sticky Sticky." Momma got so mad and said I wasn't watching Stick. She asked Jesus to find him.

Momma tells me not to move and so at least I don't go away. I knew that was the first time we were two. Gwen and I sat and my feet went fuzzy and I feel scared. I wished I could be with Momma but she was looking for Stick in the closet. I think that we should pray to God and not Jesus. That was a mistake because Jesus didn't bring Stick back to us. Momma was crying. I heard her saying about she thought he was with me. I felt sad and mad at Stick because it's his fault and I get in trouble. I know what to do when I get lost by accident. I go to the front of the grocery store to wait for Momma or I tell a man dressed like a policeman who watches for people who are stealing from the store to find her for me. I don't talk to strangers. The stranger will be super nice and have candy. He has a big smile that is nice. Or sometimes he has a big white van with puppies inside that I want to see except I am not allowed to say that I want to see them even if I do. The stranger isn't the policeman or the lady who gets to push all the buttons on the cash register that counts our groceries. Stick doesn't know anything like that.

Gwen said to me that we should go out of the cottage and we

sneak out the door and onto the rock and it smells like warm and I see the water is twinkling at me and the dock looks like a tongue stuck out. I walked over to step on the tongue.

"Hi."

"Hi, dock."

The dock didn't answer.

"Hello, dock!"

"Nana?"

It didn't sound like it came from the dock if the dock could talk and I didn't think yes. I looked down and it was almost dark and it was Stick tucked behind the side of the rock. It was a big round rock. Even bigger than his head and body. It was hard to see him because of his shirt that is like the color of the rock and everything is round.

"Is that you, Stick?"

"Hi."

"What are you doing?"

He didn't say anything. He looked at me and then looked out at the water. I turned to look at the same place. All I saw was the lake and the sparkles and the trees that were far away on the other side and pointing up like arrows at their tops.

"Daddy," said Stick.

And because I speak Stick I knew what he was doing. He thought Daddy was coming. I looked out at the lake and no boat. I didn't see Daddy but I want Daddy and I wait to see if I can see him. I love seeing Daddy because he picks me up and swings me around really fast and like I'm going to fly into the sky but I don't. He hangs onto under my armpits and woooo up and down and up and then big squeezy hug with both arms. He sticks prickly whiskers in my neck and hot breath and laughs and says he missed me so so much. And then he does Stick next except smaller woos because Stick got scared once and started to cry even though it was just supposed to be a happy hello. I can tell he wants a Daddy hug. He got lost because he missed Daddy and decided to wait for the boat. He must be coming soon. Even though we left Daddy on purpose and Stick didn't know. I can't wait to see Daddy.

19.

I need to pee so I go out of our tree fort and I sit near the stump. My pee isn't very much. I kick dirt over it and go back to the fort. Stick is under the tree and it stinks now so I look in and he has peed a little inside.

"Stick!" I yell so mad.

"What?"

"That's my spot."

"Nana?"

"You peed in my spot."

He looks at his little pool of pee but it's like he doesn't care. I am getting sick of Stick because he thinks all his problems are my problems because he just stares at everything and won't do anything. I get so mad that both my hands are in fists and I go grrrr.

"Get it out," I yell.

He looks at the pee and it's like he doesn't even think he put it there. He is making me do everything and he just sits like a stump and then he sticks out one finger like he is going to touch it. I almost tell him no but then I don't care. He puts his finger in the pee and then pulls it back because he knows only after he sticks his finger that it is gross and wipes it on his pj top.

"Use dirt and put it over on top," I tell him. I have to have every idea as if I'm the momma. He looks at me and then looks to the side of our fort and sees the tree that I dragged to make a wall. He pulls on it and breaks off only a tiny stick and pokes that in the pee. He stirs it around like that is going to get out of my spot. I am so mad I feel like my head is so red it will be a volcano explosion off the top of my neck.

"You are too stupid to cover up pee," I yell at him with my scary voice. I take a rock and I use it like a shovel and I put dirt over the pee so it is down lower in the floor of the fort. "You are stupid stupid stupid."

I have to scrape the needles out with a flat rock to get the pee all disappeared and it is so gross that I feel barf in my neck. It comes up almost but not all the way.

"Stupid Stick," I yell and finally the pee is gone so I can sit again. And Stick's eyes are wet and I see a tear leaking out but I don't care.

But then his bum is dirty and he stands up and shows it to me.

"Help me, Nana," he says.

"Arrrgh," I scream in his face and he shrinks back like he is scared and that is good because he better be because arrrgh and I am bigger and can punch him anytime I want. No one is here to stop me. I stamp out and stamp over and tell him to sit down outside the fort. He tries to bring his inside dog and walks up on his hands and knees with his head down and his tongue out but I don't care. He smiles like we are friends but we aren't. He stinks and I really hate having a brother ever. He tries to give me a paw and even does a few barks but he sees that I don't want his inside dog and I don't care. He whimpers more and goes off to sit in the fort.

"No," I shout. "No going in the fort. Bad Sticky."

His eyes look sad and I don't care either.

I need to watch for the black dog and I keep looking around. I want to know when he will be back. I don't know but I better get my weapons ready because dust for fairies is not big enough for the power. I wander around looking for the right stick and finally after a long time I find it. It is big enough to hold in my hand like thicker than my thumb and almost as big as my wrist. I find another that is bigger like almost thicker than my leg but I have to use two hands to pick it up. That is no good because it would be hard to sneak up on the black dog and I will be right there before I could stab and if I made a mistake he can just reach and bite me. Instead I need a stick that I can throw like a spear and that's how I know the right stick is exactly right. I try to throw it a few times and it hits the dirt and bounces off and lies on its side. I try again and the same thing happens and so that's how I know I need to make the end into a pointy. It will stick into the dirt and into the black dog.

I have a flat rock and that is good because I can scrape the stick on it to make a point. I wish I had a big long knife because then I could put it on the end and already have a point because I start scraping and my arms burn fast. But I don't want black dog to come when I am not ready so I keep scraping. I find a flatter rock with an edge and pick it up and yuck it is the pee rock and

I say grrrr at Stick who is sitting near the fort and ignoring me. I wipe my hands on the ground and find another rock and it is better so I use it to scrape the point and it works. I put the stick between my feet to hold it and sit on the needles and I scrape and then little shaves of wood come off the stick. In a long time and I have to take breaks but then I get a good point again.

I test it and it sticks a little bit more into the ground. I see Stick sitting there like a lump on the ground. He has two small sticks that are no good even though he thinks they are cars. If they are cars they don't go fast. I do a big roar and Stick turns around and his eyes are puffy but they still go big and he looks scared and all he does is cry. Stupid Stick. He will be no good when black dog comes it will be all up to me and everything is up to me. I turn away and stab at the ground and I find a softer part where I can stick in the stick and make it stay and I practice. Over and over I roar like a daddy and I pretend the spot is black dog and he is scared and I get him dead. And I am the queen of the land and no one else can be.

20.

I scrub my hands on the ground because something is wrong with the skin. I wait for the sun to come and warm me up and it won't. And I was sitting on my sharpening rock and I found a bubble between my fingers. I think the black dog spit on me and made my skin go on fire and now it is melting off. Sometimes skin is itchy when it melts and it feels really bad. There are a few more bubbles that I find up my arm. I rub them on the ground because maybe if that part of the skin comes off faster with rubbing it would feel better. My skin gone will make me sad but there is always skin underneath like a scab. Maybe I will get blood and this would be worth a Band-Aid even if there was no blood and I think Momma would say yes. Or she might say it is the one that needs air. When I am sure it is a cut that needs a Band-Aid and Momma often says no it's one that needs air. I see Sticky out of the corner of my eye but I don't feel like talking to him because I am so itchy itchy itchy.

"Nana?" Stick says. I can tell by the way he stands back and says my name that he knows I am still mad about the pee.

"Nana?" he says again.

"What?" I don't look at him. I am looking at my hand. One of the bubbles has popped so that will feel better. There is not blood but instead it is yellow blood that is running from the bubble to my arm. It is gross and yuck. I hope it will feel better because it is popped and running and still too itchy. Stick comes right in front of me and looks too.

"Band-Aid?" he asks.

We both always wonder when we get Band-Aids.

"I don't know."

"Owey."

"What?"

He turns and doesn't take his pants off because his pants are gone. On his bum is red and bubbles all over. The black dog has spit on him very much all over.

"It's spit."

"Owey, Nana."

"Bubble bum," I say.

"Not fat." He turns and puts his eyebrows down at me.

"You have bubbles on your bum. The black dog spit on you with his gob and it is eating your skin off your bum."

"Eeeeeee. Bitchy," he says and he reaches behind to his bum to scratch.

We both feel really itchy on our skin and inside our whole bodies and we try to scratch and Sticky starts to cry. I wish he didn't because I want to cry too. I am a big girl and even though I always cry when Momma tells me to stop I can't. I cry when we pick up Daddy because I hadn't seen him in a long time.

Momma says don't cry when someone hasn't seen you because all they remember is that you cry. Not as much that you smile. I still cry and Momma says that she knows we have hard things and she has hard things too. But she says that Daddy is coming and we will all be better now. She says that if you go past the things that are hard you can be so so strong.

Stick lets out a little noise but he doesn't cry and we sit under the tree. I am so cold a bit shaky but kind of hot and I don't feel so good. Stick doesn't either and he doesn't say because no English in his brain worms but he goes on his knees and crawls closer to me. He puts his head in my lap and I remember I peed my pants because of the black dog and it stinks but Stick doesn't care. He lies down and whimpers again like Snoopy and shuts his eyes and I put my hand on him like Momma would.

"It's okay," I say.

I am so so hungry. I hope it is like that day when we woke up and it was Daddy Day because Momma started to get things ready at the cottage to make a cake and she let us lick the spoon. And Momma let me lick the spoon because we made cake and Daddy was coming to the cottage to be in our family. Maybe it was a mistake that we left him by accident. And we were going to eat the cake. But not the beaters because she doesn't have a beater at the cottage where you pop out the silver part and lick it. She just stirs with her arm. I got sad about that but then I got to lick the bowl and only give Stick a few dips with his finger so I felt better. We made the cake and I wanted a piece but we had to wait and then I was sad again. But then we got to go swimming in the lake to wash off because we had chocolate on us and all on our faces. Stick had it on both cheeks and some on his forehead even from when he tried to stick his head in the bowl and I stopped him because only a few finger licks. But maybe he snuck around my back because there was even chocolate on his ears and I don't know how it got there. We duck into the lake and it was cold and the sun was warm and it felt nice. The lake scrubbed us off and we put on just T-shirts over our bathing suits because Daddy will want to swim so we are already ready.

"Hungry, Nana," says Stick.

I pat his head so his inner dog feels nice. "Me, too, Stick."

I am hungry. I remember I saw Daddy's paddle lying on the beach and broken. I don't know how to fix a paddle. It is on the beach on the island and I don't even know where that is anymore. I saw it from far away. Momma tied on our life jackets and we got to sit in the very front of the boat in a seat that is squishy but there was a crack that bites my leg so I put Stick on that side. When I sit the life jacket goes up nearer my ears but on Stick it puts him in a headlock and he has to have a strap that goes under his dingle and I'm glad I don't have that anymore. I love the smell of gas so I sniff it when the boat starts and Stick puts his arms in the air and yells "Yay" because he loves the boat. Stick looks the wrong way so I punch him and point to the dock and he yells and tries to stand up but he's not allowed. I pull him back to the seat and he tips over because a life jacket is stuffed under his chin.

"Can you get him, Anna?"

I know Momma meant I should watch Stick in the boat. I tipped him right way up and I looked back and Momma was smiling and she said "Thank you" and looked so pretty and happy. I knew that she loved me so much and that I found Stick by the dock when he was lost. And that's how we remembered to get Daddy.

"Go home," says Stick.

I want to go home too. I want to eat cake. I want to look out and see Daddy standing on the dock. He is not in two pieces he is in just one piece and his eyebrows and darker skin than me and big white teeth and smile that makes me warm. I know that Stick thinks Daddy just stands on the dock waiting for us the whole time. That's why Stick was watching the lake. And he thinks that Daddy stands behind the garden gate waiting until dinnertime when he comes back through to see us and eat. But when I look at Daddy standing from far away on the dock I think I don't know how long he has been standing there and it might be a really long time. Even though we didn't let him in the car he found a way to get to the dock and that's why his smile is so big. Maybe he came before the nighttime and was standing there and the cottage only has one phone and postcards from Grandpa. When Grandpa calls on the phone I am supposed to say to him that Daddy is not there or he is working but not that Daddy is not in our family. It is a secret. He is still in our family he is just not there because of a break and Grandpa doesn't need to know. And maybe if Stick is right and Daddy was standing for too long on the dock he got scared in the night standing there but he didn't know we would find him but we did and so everything is okay.

I want to go home. Momma pulls the boat away from the dock really slow after we make cake and lick spoons and wash off to be clean. We got through rocks and past Mr. and Mrs. Henderson's house and they are sitting on their dock with books and they both look happy and wave. When the lake gets bigger we speed up but it's not as fast as Daddy goes so I am happy we are getting him. When I see Daddy on the dock he has work clothes on but except he has taken off the shirt and put on a T-shirt for the cottage. His hair looks more shaggy and I think he changed but not too much. His briefcase is at his feet and that makes me worry because I know inside is papers that will make my momma huff and glasses that make Daddy huff when I touch them. Also my pens and special pocket for paper so when I need to do work I have it there and can reach it but not other things because they are too important. I look at the dock and Daddy is still waving and now I see he has the biggest smile and many teeth show out loud on his face because he is really happy that we remembered. And he likes cake and maybe he knows it is chocolate. Daddy doesn't like to be away from us but we forgot him.

"He is at work," I told Stick because I know that's what he will believe and even though he was gone from us for longer and I'm not allowed to tell Grandpa or Stick or the summer friends even though I knew he was gone.

Daddy sees us when we are still far away and that is because Momma drives the boat slow because she always does and because we are near the marina and you are not supposed to make super waves to knock all the boats around. This is stupid because the funnest part is the big waves that make Stick and I go whoa whoa. But I am not allowed to say stupid so I don't say it I just look up and see Daddy. He has a big smile on his face and an arm over his head that is going back and forth to say hello. It is so far away I don't know if it is Daddy and then I know it is because sometimes I can just tell and Momma yells over the motor "Can you see your dad?"

"Home, Nana," says Stick.

Stick looks so sad and my heart drips again. I have worry that we didn't forget Daddy this time. He went away on his own and isn't here because of different things. Maybe he is standing on the dock and waiting with a big smile but we are not coming for him because we don't have a boat and I don't have Momma near me. I can't get Daddy and so we are not together and it is my fault. The paddle is broken and I don't know where it is.

"Don't worry, Daddy," I whisper with my hand on Stick's head and under the tree and near the fort but nothing else that I know where it is. "We are coming."

I see Momma on the dock and Daddy grabs the rope and they hug for a really long time. They kiss and I start to cry and I don't know why but it is my heart dripping. Stick tries to climb out of the boat for hugs. I have to pull his life jacket because he can fall into the crack between and get into the water and smooshed by the boat. I pull him back and he screams at me to stop. He wants to hug Daddy. I want to hug Daddy and Momma too but they are hugging each other and Daddy is saying things to Momma's ear and I don't want them to stop because then maybe we are always together even though I want a hug soon. I look at them and it is our family with two parents and two kids and we are supposed to be like that. We went and got Daddy and it made everyone so so happy again. We were four.

21.

We are only two just Stick and me only. I feel scared that the black dog is coming soon and look to the open grassy wet and that isn't a place I know. We waited in the forest and it's not the spot either.

"We need to find Daddy, Stick."

"Okey."

"We need to go."

Stick doesn't answer. I look farther away and there is a line that goes into the bush and it's like a trail that Daddy makes around the cottage for walks. A path. There is one from the boat to the cottage but you can go longer around the whole way and that is long. I can do it but Stick can't make it without a carry. I can do it but I will need to watch out for snakes because Daddy or Momma goes first to watch. I can surprise a snake but a grown-up sees a snake before it gets surprised.

Stick is scratching his bum on the ground and I wish he had

pants for the important hike but he needs to go with no pants. I pull on the back of my pj's because they are showing my bum smile. We take water on hikes in bottles and Stick and I don't have bottles. I wave him over and he follows me but his feet are draggy. He is going so slow and the black dog could catch him in one step. I bend down and drink from the puddle and I scoop chocolate milk water in my hands for Stick. He tries to hang his tongue out like his inside dog but he doesn't really think it lives inside him this time. He licks up a little from my hands and it feels better on my hands so I stick them in the puddle and the mud is better. I scoop muck up and put it on my hands and arms and I think aaaaah. It doesn't itch for one second and phew. Stick is watching me and even though I still don't like him I tell him to turn around and I take a big scoop of muck and tell him to stay still. He screams really loud and runs away because he thinks I will beat him in a mud fight. I don't care because there is all the mud for me.

I find bubbles on my legs and arms when I scrunch up my pj's and I cover all the places with mud. It feels better that way and a little cold but the mud is warm and it will soak through to my bones and is making me better and taking away the powers from the black dog spit. I am all mud and I get up to find my spear to keep the black dog away because I don't want any more spit on my skin or it will melt off and I will be only bones like at the museum hanging on wires. I get it in my hand and try once more to spear. I let out a big roar and I spear down. No bones!

"Rwooooooooooooar," I say and I know I can beat the black dog and I must find where Daddy is waiting. I don't know this time if that is at the dock and the cottage or Toronto.

I hear sniffy sounds and Sticky is crouched down like Snoopy in trouble and looks like he thinks I will hit him. Like maybe I saw Mrs. Buchanan swat with a magazine rolled into a tube like inside paper towel but she says to Momma she didn't.

"I can get the black dog," I tell Stick.

He sniffles again because he thinks he is a dog and maybe I have magazines in rolls and I see that he doesn't know English enough with too many worms in his head to know what I am saying. And he was asleep so he doesn't know about the enemy and babies don't know even though he is not really a baby anymore.

"Come on," I say. "We are going."

He whimpers again. "Go?"

I think Stick wants to know where. I try to think and I close my eyes and remember before I ever played with Barbie and Momma got so mad for me begging. I used to be a good girl and Momma ran my bath at nighttime. She checked the water and told me to put a foot in and say if it was right and so many bubbles came up to my chin. We played for a long time for so long and I had a boat and Momma helped me make a river through all the bubbles so my boat could get through on a journey. We played a lot of things. She stirred up the water for more bubbles. We made me a beard and new hair out of bubbles that stuck up with horns. She lifted me up so I could see in the mirror and we laughed. The bubbles went pop pop pop and they went to bubble heaven and the water was just like gray dirt because I was at the park so much time with the sand. Momma helped me lie back and she put her hand under my head so that I could float in the water. She said that is so good I will be able to swim at the cottage in the summertime. I felt so happy and Momma hums the song and I sing our bath song with her too. She smiles and says my hair is floating like seaweed. She laughed and said she thought it was funny and she did the floating song with Grandpa when she was a little girl.

I need to be good and make us four and get back to the tub.

"Come on." I wave at Stick and start to walk the pathway and holding my spear in case of the black dog. At the end should be the cottage and I get Momma and the boat and we will go to Toronto and find our family will be four.

I walk and I want to go fast because Toronto is a long way home. I hear breathing behind me. I check quickly because of the black dog and it is Stick and I know that. He is always following me and I tell him he needs to walk faster. He moves his arms like he is walking his fastest and swinging his arms but he is going so slow and I keep saying "Hurry up." He looks sad and keeps itching. He didn't want the mud on his black dog spit place so he wouldn't let me help and it's his fault. We walk on the path and there are a lot of bushes on it that hit me in the face. I let a big one go and I hear a scream and I look back and Stick has been whacked on the head with it. I help him stand up again. I tell him not to walk so close.

I tell him to go faster to keep up. We are walking and there are very many bushes on the path and someone is not very good at making a path. I keep walking and pushing through and I feel a leaf that is wet. It shakes on me and gets my pj arm wet too. I stop and I am frozen because I don't know why it is wet and then I get scared that it maybe is spit from the black dog. Maybe he is making me follow him or I am very close. I listen very much around me because it is hard to see from all the bushes and I hear something come so I turn and hold out the spear. The bushes wiggle and then they go apart. I get so scared and my breath flies out and I go "Ha." And I see Stick pops through the leaves again.

"You are lucky I didn't stab you," I yell at him.

He has cuts on his face and he is crying and he tries to talk but I can't understand because of all this snot and it just sounds like baby talk.

"You can't sneak up at me," I yell back. I don't like him crying because that scares me too. There are more wet leaves around us. One drool goes on my forehead and one goes on my cheek and it's like the black dog is working to scare us on purpose and there is a lot of spit in his mouth because he is about to eat a feast.

I know he is close because even the black dog can't spit far. I stab into the bushes with my spear and Stick starts to scream and I need him to shut up because I can't hear the black dog and I yell at him to be quiet and he screams louder. Every time he screams I get more scared because it means I can't hear when the black dog will pounce. I stab into the bushes and I turn around and try to look all ways but I can't see. There is a dark spot and I run for it and I stab but my spear flies out of my hand and goes away. And with Stick crying and shouting the black dog knows where we are and is finding us and spitting.

The spit is like rain. And the spit starts to go into my hair I am getting wetter and wetter in the spit and soon I won't be able to move but at least Stick has stopped screaming and I can only hear him crying a little. My last chance is to get the spear in my hand and try to stab before I freeze and have to watch my body get eaten. He will start with my legs and chew them off so I won't be dead yet. He will eat my arms and chew out my belly even though it is empty. I won't get dead until he has eaten so much and it is only when he decides it is time to eat my head for dessert that the lights will go off and it's bedtime except I get dead. I push around in the leaves for my spear and I know it is here. I keep looking for a long time and each time I push away a bush and it's not there I feel more and more scared. It is raining hard and there is water all over me and I am shaking and so so cold and I think I will probably get dead.

22.

I can't find my spear and I stop looking because it is not here anymore. Near me it's only bushes. I push away from them and then there my spear is on the ground. I get it in my hand and I am glad, but then I can't see because of so many bushes. I get out to a place with mud on the ground. I am all wet and the black dog has turned everything to wet rain and is waiting. But then I see it is a stump and there are only stumps and they look dead. The dead stumps look like an army that got beat and they are all dead so they rot. The wood is like splinters down the side and there is black on them and mushrooms. I hold the spear and watch. I don't like the stumps and want to get away. It is grayer but not nighttime. It feels like a bigger monster flew into the sky and its belly is hiding the sun from me. I shiver from the cold and my kneecaps have come loose. I think they might drop onto the ground and then I will have to look for them. So they won't fall off I crouch down by one of the stumps and keep my knees bent with the caps on the top of my legs. I hug my legs. Then I look behind me for Stick. He is not there. He always follows me and I can't ever stop him most times and now he isn't there. I walk back a bit because I think he sat down on his bum. No Stick. I call him and he doesn't say anything back. I wait and I think he will come and he doesn't come. I feel a big cry in my eyes and my stomach goes around. "Stick?" I yell again and no one answers me. I am one.

I keep yelling and I stab in the bushes and I saw Stick on the path and I don't know where it is anymore. The rain is more and big drops knock on my head. I keep going through the bushes and tackle my way and it looks clear in front of me so I think I will see our fort. I push the bushes away and see the dead stumps again and I don't know why. They are in front when I left them behind me, so they jumped over my head and sat down here. It smells like wet shoes. My feet are soaked except no shoes and so just the skin is turning white and wrinkles. I shiver and the rain seems to turn up more and there is no fort. I wish I could go back to the fort if the cottage is not here. I look up and down to remember the path again and it has jumped away from me too.

I don't like it being alone. I have so much worry for Stick and I have my spear in my hand and I hold it tight but my body is feeling sleepy. I don't know if I can fight a black dog and maybe I am not a brave queen that can do a battle or even just a brave princess. I cry and cry and I think there are tears in my eyes and down my face but I don't even know because there is so much water and it is raining and that adds in with my tears and no one can see me. My snot gets out of my nose and my body does little throw-ups to push my tears out so hard. I cry and nothing makes me feel better. I know something bad has happened and I look at my hands. Gwen is not there. I don't know where she is. I try and think and stop crying to get myself back in but I can't. My whole body has gone away because I am one and that is not enough to be in a family so I am lost too. I got left behind. I need to get back because maybe they don't know I am gone. It is hard to think because the rain is banging so hard on my head. I put my head in my knees and I stare at the ground and my arms are over my head. My arms are a little bit like an umbrella but not that good. My brain can work without the banging of the drops and I think where is Gwen? Does she know I am gone or did she leave me on purpose because I was bad? And maybe she is jealous because I wanted Barbie and so so mad. I could like her to sniff even if she is wet and where is Stick? He is so warm. He was in the bushes and his face got bloody and the black dog was there. Everyone is gone. Just one and maybe one.

I have to squint out to see through the rain and I look to see if Stick or Gwen is close to me. Usually he tries to follow me all the time. He breathes and I hear it through his nose and if I stop he bangs into my bum because he follows so close. He is not beside me and he is not one of the stumps or sitting by the stumps. I stand up and look from higher but there is no Sticky. I know that he is scared and he doesn't like rain and he will really want me like I want Gwen but no one has anyone anymore. The rain comes more and it beats me back down to hugging my knees and I cry harder now because Sticky can't even hug his knees and stay on his feet because he is too fat. I don't know where he is.

Electric lightning starts. There is a flash everywhere and someone has turned on the lights and there are not lights. It flicks once and twice and God is making the lights show everything around me that looks like the black dog but it is not except I'm not sure because the electric lightning blinks too fast on and off on and off and I can't see. I see it like knives in the sky and I am not supposed to be outside. It might hit my head because there are only stumps and I am a little bit taller. And the electric goes again and I hear the angels banging and I know they are very mad and God is mad because Stick is gone and I am very bad because I lost him and that is what I was supposed to do is watch.

"Stick!" I shout.

I listen but I don't hear him not even whining. I want to call Gwen too but she can't walk without me to carry her.

"Sticky! Stick!" I stand up and the rain hits me on every side of my body and I shout both his names over and over and my throat has claws that are ripping me and I am so scared and my kneecaps wiggle so much they will fall and my tummy heaves and I have a little barf and my arms are so bubbled and red and my face is hot and might fall off but I have to keep calling and I shout for Stick for the longest time I can. And finally I can't shout because my voice isn't making noise out of my throat. My legs fall down and I am on the ground and my heart has shaken loose and rolled away. I can't open my eyes. All I see is my lids and black and I can barely feel the rain but the itchy black is eating up my skin from the outside and crawling all through my blood. I want to get up but I can't. Only my brain can think so everything is black and I can't move. He has pushed me over and is eating my insides and melting away my skin. The black dog is inside me.

23.

I am one. My body is wet and it is dark and I can feel my teeth are jumping in my mouth because they want to get away from the black dog. They are very scared. The rain is falling on my body and I roll and it won't stop. I am so cold and the hole in my stomach is gone because the rain filled it up. I am empty except the space is getting so full of water that you can see right through me and a goldfish could swim anywhere in my body and not get stuck. The stumps are all around me and the fish is not here.

I think of where Momma and Daddy are. When I was with them we paddled in the canoe and I sat on top of Coleman because he takes up so much room in the canoe. Stick and Daddy were singing near the front of the canoe because Momma is the best at paddling and goes in the back with me and Coleman. The canoe rocked a little and the water was chop chop chop. I needed to get off Coleman and down in the canoe in front of

Momma so weight comes off the top and doesn't make us so tipsy. Momma put her paddle across the edges of the canoe and folded her sweatshirt for the bottom so it didn't hurt my bum. She helped me slide off Coleman because he is so big and he has to fit sideways in between the bars to fit so it is a long way. I like the canoe with Momma because I have her all for me and no Stick close by. We were close to the island and she looked at the map and picks a place on this side because the moon is nearly full and that is when it is round with no dents. She and I talked a lot too. She said "We are four again."

And the rain has stopped and it is so dark. It is dark inside my eyes and through my eye crack. I think I am dead so nothing matters but something is squishy on my face. I am lying on the ground and curled into a ball. I am so cold it is a freezer. There is no thunder or electric lightning anymore. It is silent like after a storm and that is more quiet than anything else. I was in between Momma and Daddy after the lightning at the first night in the tent. I wish I was there again even though I was so scared because the bang was right above our head. When Momma counted there was no more numbers between the light and the bang and that's how we knew the storm was right there. Momma and Daddy and me lay on our backs and had the sleeping bag tucked up so much it didn't even touch the sides of the blue tent. Stick was pushed at the other side of the tent and sleeping and that was nice for me. We stared at the ceiling of the tent and we could see the branches of the trees bobbing around. The rain sounded like it was dropping onto a raincoat and that is one of my favorite things. The drops went slower. Daddy said in a whisper voice that it was so dark the moon was still climbing up and I didn't know where it went but it was so quiet I didn't want to make my voice out loud. We lay there and listened to the rumbles get softer and less drops and they traveled off to across the lake and there are no other tents so to a land far away and we kept listening and I didn't even move or wiggle and we listened until they were all gone.

Momma even fell asleep but the snoring was from Sticky not her. Daddy put his finger to his lips to tell me shh and picked me up with his muscles like I was a baby. Normally I'm not a baby anymore but I was snuggled on his shoulder and no one could see so it was nice to be the baby. Daddy put a blanket around us like Batman's cape so I'd be warm. He walked out through the zip door. His chin and the whiskers were there and they would grow because he is on our holiday. His feet on the needles were soft and he was walking on our campsite toward the lake. He laughed a little rumble in his chest that I hear because my ear was smooshed against it and warm. He stood on the edge of the beach and I knew because I could hear the water lick at the stones and I could smell it being warm and deep too. I could hear a creaking that sounds like a sad ghost and Daddy said it was just a tree feeling old and grumpy. And he told me "Look" and I turned my head even though I like his warm chest on my cheek and looked out and there was a big moon that was hanging above the water like it might fall in but it didn't. It just hung and looked like the glitteriest gold and it had a big long tail that is stretching across the top of the water and came to reach Daddy's toes. He stood there and we both looked and it was like the moon was talking through the light and saying things about love.

"The tail looks like a path across the water," he said. "We can follow it and get to the moon."

And Daddy said he was so happy to be with us and that we were in Algonquin Park and that was a good way to be four.

I open my eye crack and roll and I am soaked and my teeth are jumpy. I see something peek up through the trees and I can see it is the moon. It is hanging and round with just one side a little bit slanted like it got a small bang too. I see it shine in my eyes and even though I am so cold it makes my bones a little more warm and my eyes are dropping again and I am too tired but I know what the moon says and so I nod a little with one cheek scraped on the ground.

"I'll come."

24.

My eye cracks see light and I open them again for the moon but this time it is light and there is smoke all around. I think it is a fire and I sit right up. My head is pounding and what happened to the moon? I look for it straight ahead. It is gone and I feel empty but then I think I know where it was. I can go there still and be close for when it comes back because it always does and I can take the path. I try to stand up and my legs are floppy and like pipe cleaners except not as fuzzy. I have to use my hands to get them in the right place to keep me up. I see my spear on the ground and I want to pick it up so I have to use my hands again to bendy my knees and get it. I try and hold the spear up but it feels too heavy and I keep looking up so that I can remember when I saw the moon and so I can walk to meet it. The spear keeps tilting to the ground and stabbing but not a lot so I let it. I take a step forward. I balance on the spear and it is like an old man and that's what

I am now because I am all alone. I take a step and I move my spear forward and that's how my feet know how to follow. I point my spear to where the moon used to be and I hope will be again and take more steps.

Bang

I hear a loud noise. It goes again like a firecracker except that it is not a black sky to see lights and there is no party.

Bang

It is a gun. It goes again or maybe like the hunter is coming and he has a gun. The black dog may have been running from the hunter too now he is inside me. I wonder if the hunter will try and shoot me.

Bang

And I know the hunter has a gun.

Bang

This is a naughty hunter who uses his gun too much. I don't have a gun or shoes so I feel so scared. I keep walking and I bump into a stump and that was the wrong way if the stump was there so I turn and go the other way. I want to run but my legs won't let me run. My throat must have the blisters now too because it feels so sore I can't swallow like normal not even for food. I put a foot down and another foot in front of that and I can't hear the hunter at all. I wonder if there is any food left and so I hope he doesn't eat the rest of the cookies because he is hungry after a battle with the black dog. I hope he leaves some for me even though I have no shoes. I feel sores all on my body. I don't think Momma has enough Band-Aids so I will keep just walking without any. I have a think about the black dog and how he lives in my tummy now and he growls. That explains why it is hard to move because he is heavy so I must go slow. Once he lives in my stomach he won't want to leave so I will need to carry him and it's okay but heavy.

I keep walking and the black dog is with me and I guess he likes walking to the moon because he starts to feel softer. I feel something on my back and I turn and there is a little peek of light coming through the trees. The sun is reaching his arms through the trees and trying to warm everybody up. He puts a hand on my face and I turn to keep walking and he smiles on my back.

"Thank you," I say quiet.

I feel better because I am not just one if the black dog is with me. I sit on the ground for a minute to make my head think. I put my hand on my stomach to pat the black dog and we have a little talk. The black dog is quiet and talks in a soft voice. I don't have to have so much worry. I feel better when I sit and maybe he is helping me be okay. He says the hunters have stopped and they are not hungry anymore so no guns that we can hear. He says that I was very bad because I wanted too many Barbies. I lost Sticky. Last time I lost Stick Momma was looking in the closet and I found him. Then that made Momma remember we left Daddy. He came back. He said we were going to walk on the path to the moon. Momma said "We will be there." She means the moon.

I need to find Stick. I will look for a long time always forever. That is first. I stand up and start walking and my body is feeling warmer and the black dog starts to purr kind of like a grrrr gaaaa but softer. Kind of like a cat but a scary growl too so I know that even though he is there he will sometimes be nice to me when I am doing what he wants and being a good girl. He purrs louder and I keep moving my feet even though it's so hard but my spear goes forward and I keep it in my hand. The black dog is even happier and the purr is loud. I know that I need to keep walking to keep him like that. There is a snort in the purr and what if there is two black dogs? There is one in my tummy and he says he is just the one. But I still hear the other purr and I am bad so the hunter is coming to get me now? The purr sounds more like a man and I think maybe the hunter ate everything and he saw smoke coming from my head and they are going to get me and creep through the bushes on their toes so I don't see. I stop and listen and it does sound like a big man who is making the noises and pretending to trick me so I use my hands to bend my knees more so I am ready.

And then I worry that the hunter got Stick. I need to rescue Stick from the hunter and I miss Stick so much and I wish he never went away. I want to see him so we can go and get Momma and Daddy. I love Stick and I need to save him. I feel sick because I didn't watch and it is my fault. I will never ever not watch Stick again and I tell that to God if he helps me find him. I try to hold up my spear and my arm is floppy. I see that God is not going to help so I try asking Jesus. He is a carpenter and could make me a real sword so I ask for that and nothing. I ask again and remember please and he doesn't say anything and all I have is me and the black dog in my belly and there is nothing else.

I know the hunter is very smart. I put my spear on my shoulder and that is better and I can stab him fast from here and get Stick from him if my arm will listen. I take a step forward so maybe they will see my bare toes. I have to push some of the bushes out of the way and I know they will see my bush pushing and maybe I will see theirs so I watch like I have eagles in my eyes but I see a bush wiggle around me. I take another step and there is a bush wiggle just ahead. It is a wiggle enough to know the hunter is hiding and has Stick trapped as his prisoner. I get the spear up and watch the wiggle and it must be the hunter is hiding down in the bottom of the bush because I can't see him at all and he is very sneaky.

I think the hunter is too sneaky but the black dog in my belly gives a rumble and I think yes it is okay. I put my hand on the black dog one more time and I know he will help. I will stab my spear in as hard as I can and scare the hunter enough and then start a battle and the black dog will jump out to fight beside me. Or I have a worry that the black dog will jump out and get me dead and I'm not sure which one. But I have to save Stick so I need to try and not have worry. But then I start to get scared about what is going to happen and if I start to shake it will be too late. I open my mouth and then put out a big roar and I think that I should do that second and do my spear first but I can already hear the roar but it isn't so loud. I make it louder and I lift the spear and I chuck it into the bushes as hard as I can and it goes in pretty good. It spears into a soft part of the mud and stands up and I feel a little happy because that means it stuck.

I must have got the hunter dead through the heart and he can't move or anything. Quiet and no bushes are moving or talking. He is not around and there is only one hunter because they creep through the bushes apart from each other and I don't hear any others. But his friends might not see because they aren't coming to help or else this is a hunter that maybe has no friends. I stick out my foot for a step and push the bush and I see the spear is in the ground and I feel a little sad because there's no dead hunter. The black dog does not jump out to help. I pull to get my spear back from the ground. It comes out and then I take a step and my bare foot hits something. I pull my foot back and my hair goes prickle and I feel scared and look down. I have stepped on a leg that is sticking out from the bushes. If it is a hunter's leg then maybe but I don't think it is because there's no boots. I take a step back and my hair is all prickled even on my arms and I want to run but my legs won't move fast enough. I think the black dog will jump out of me for a feast and maybe on me because he is so hungry and only likes me when I'm brave. But he doesn't jump again and he keeps purring and doesn't move. So I am stuck in place with a black dog and feet that are stuck in one spot and I look at the leg that is lying on the ground and it is small. I reach with my spear and I push it and the skin pushes in so much.

"Stick?"

I push again and the purring stops and there is a snort. And I hear a quiet voice. "Ow."

"Stick?" I say again and I push the bush to the side and it is Stick lying in the dirt and I start to cry because I am so happy to see his little squishy face. He is the dirtiest baby I have ever seen but a little part of yellow is sticking out and I see the ducks on his pj top and no bottoms just his dirty dingle. I think he is dead because he doesn't move and he is bubbled and puffy and red and doesn't look like he did when he was alive. But then I hear another snort and he tries to open his eye up a little. I drop my spear and grab him and get his little body in my arms and it is floppy. I give him the biggest hug ever and I cry and cry. I never know how much I miss him all the times.

"Nana?"

I think he says my name but his English is more bad which

means I am the only person on the whole entire earth that can understand him. It is up to me to save him because no one else can and he knows. I put his little arms around me and hold him close to my body. I look at him and he doesn't see back and his eyelids look like a ham that Momma brings on picnics and cuts into slices with a knife. He is gucky and gross and I will love him anyway. I grab his arm and spin him over and he flops on his back and I check for blood.

"No blood," I say.

Normally he would say there was because he wants a Band-Aid but this time he doesn't say anything. He just lets out a little moan and a snore-purr and I think it sounds like he is breathing harder than normally. I will save him. I will bring him to Momma and Daddy at the moon.

I try and get him to stand up but he is so floppy. He is standing less than Gwen and I miss her and wish I could sniff. I get him on his feet and try to get him to hold the spear to walk. His feet are all bubbled and they are big so he can't really step. Sometimes he would like to have bigger feet but they look like they hurt and are not comfortable slippers. I feel sad for his bigger feet like that. I will save him and the sun reaches in and tells me to try to just get to the moon and it will help in my bones and pushing my back. I try to carry him like Momma by grabbing under his arms and putting his legs on my waist. I can walk a few steps but I fall and drop him. He doesn't cry or say he will tell Momma. He just flops on the ground. I get down and look at him and his face looks like someone put a pig mask over the top but I can still see my brother. I am his person in the world and I feel my muscles have enough sun so they get warm and strong and I am like a battery and my robot can go.

"Stick?"

He turns his head a little.

"We are going to the moon, okay?"

I see his eyes inside the pig eyes move just a little and I know that means he wants to go because he wants to see Momma and Daddy and will try as much as he can. I have to leave my spear behind and even though the black dog no longer purrs he wants to make me strong and he boils inside my body and bursts into a roar. I drag Stick by the foot to a rock and I push him up on it and he is almost sitting. I keep him there with one hand and turn so my back is facing him for a piggyback.

"Grab my shoulders," I say and I wiggle my hips between his legs.

He doesn't grab but his body flops forward against mine and I feel his hot cheek is between my shoulders. I grab back for a floppy arm and pull it forward over my neck and hook it like he is strangling me and normally he is not allowed but this one time he is. I get my fists under his knees and stand until I can get my hands together. I try to stand up straighter, but Stick starts to flop back. I lean over so he is lying on me and my back like a mattress but my legs are straight. I take one step and it is hard to pick up a foot and make it go forward. I close my eyes and I ask the black dog to help and I lock my knees like a robot. I start to walk.

My eyes are pointing at the ground. I have to remember to face where the moon goes. It is hard because I can barely peek up to see trees but then I see a flat part under my feet. It is a path. I glance up and see the path goes over to the trees so this must be how people get to the moon. I am glad because I can stare at the ground and keep a foot going forward and the other foot and know that I am going the right way because I can see the path. And it is hard because bushes are thwacking at me and pushing my legs. I see that they have scratched in blood to my legs and at the sides. I would like to stop and see the blood but I don't think I'll have enough batteries to get Stick on my back and I can't really stop moving my feet or I will fall so I step step step.

I step forever the longest time and I try to think how far until I get to the moon. Then I know the moon isn't up yet. I will go as far as I can until I am at the edge and need to wait for the moon and that is when I can have my muscles get less sore. I watch my one foot come to the place that I can see it with my eyes and it disappears. My other foot comes into my eyes and each time it's like there is a new cut but I can't feel it. My blood has run out from the cuts and now it's just batteries in my body. Instead of bones all the batteries are what make my leg look like a shape under the bubbles and the red and the blood. More steps and the bushes go away thank goodness. I see the needles are under my feet and they don't prickle this time. I don't feel them. All I can feel is the hot Stick on my back and his head is turned to the side so his cheek is still squished on my back and he is purring again. I take a harder step and he snorts a little and then goes back to purring so I know the black dog wants me to do this so I'll keep going and won't make him mad. I feel sad that he can tell me what to do like that but not sad because he just wants to help me with Stick and so I step step step.

There are more needles and the path is softer but still enough to see my feet on it. I take a step and something is close to my toe. I look and it is an ear and I see Gwen! She is lying on the ground and she is soaked and looks so sad but she can curl her black thread at me and I know she is okay. I don't know how she knows to go to the moon but she must have gotten here to be in the path to find me. I stop my feet and I put an arm out to grab her and Stick snorts. I feel him roll to the side. My foot slips and I have to hang onto his legs to balance and we wobble except we don't quite fall and the black dog checks my battery and says I better go because not that much. Now I am standing right over Gwen and I look down at her and no sniffs from here but I miss her. I want to squeeze her but right now I am doing a job. There is no extra hands for her.

"I love you, Gwen," I say and I step.

I step again and my toes come forward and Gwen is gone from my eyes and I am walking away.

I keep walking through trees and there are some plants and I think they are the kind that have the dangle berries. I look to the side but there are no dangle berries on these ones so I feel sad but my foot still steps. There is more dirt and a rock. I have to step over that and so hard but I do. And I see the lid of the cookies and my heart leaps because I think I want a cookie very much but then the tin is not there and I know they are gone and so oh well. I keep going and it's a little bit downhill and my feet slip forward but I can stand up more and that is better because my back was about to drop through to the ground. I take a breath and I have to take one last step down the hill and I can see pebbles and that makes it harder to balance. Before I walk on the pebbles I am straight because of the hill I hear something soft like a brushing and I make my eyes look up while they still can and it is water! I can see a lake and I am so thirsty and this is where the moon will make a trail to follow when it comes. I look to the side and I know it is the right place because there is a canoe that has fallen partway into the water and is sitting beside sticks. It is a little bit sunk but I know it is from the last person that came to find the moon and they left the canoe because they could walk the path along the water. I stop the steps and my legs bend without my meaning to and my knees go crunch into the pebbles. Stick is still purring and I try to roll him off my back and he flops and bangs his head but he doesn't cry. I look at him and his puffy face doesn't move. I feel scared that now he is dead again.

"Stick." I get right up next to his ear and whisper to him. "We did it. The moon is coming."

I watch his eyes and I don't see them move under the lids and I take one of his hands and mine are bubbled. I can't feel his skin but then I feel a little and his thumb moves and it squeezes on mine.

I get down to the lake and stick my face in and take a big drink and I am very glad about that. My throat hurts to drink it but my tongue keeps asking for more and then I get some in my hands. I try to pour it into Stick's mouth. I miss and it goes on his face but I see his tongue waggle around like it is the only part of him to like water. I get some more and watch his happy tongue and I do it again but then his tongue must have enough because it stops waggling. His bum and legs look so sore and there is dirt. I take off my pj top and it is not red but more like purple but I put it over him like a blanket. All we have to do is wait long enough for the moon. Stick feels hot but he is shaking a little and so I don't know if he is hot or cold but he doesn't need to make his worms speak English for me to know that he wants me close. Because I am his big sister. I lie behind him and curl my knees around and I put my arm over him and my hand on his chest and I give him a little squeeze.

"I love you, Stick."

And he doesn't answer but I know he hears me in his ears because I feel his heart go thump. I feel thump thump of Stick's heart and I hang on.

25.

"Anna? Alex? Are you the Whyte kids?"

My name. I put my head up and there is a man in the lake and he has a paddle in his hand and is sitting in the middle of a canoe. He is jumping out and bang on the canoe and his paddle throws onto the dirt and he makes a gaspy noise. He has a mustache and I don't like it. Like a dead caterpillar crawled up on his lip so I put my head back down. But then I lift my head again and I think he must be a stranger so I hang onto floppy Stick extra tight. I should answer because manners and I don't know. The stranger's eyes are wide and I see that his mouth is like an O and he is rushing out of the canoe and his breath is almost huffy and I think he is mad and then I see he is crying from his eyes and his face is wet and he is trying to talk.

"Oh, my God. It's the kids."

The man rushes to us and I feel scared but I can't run. The stranger would have a smile not cry so I just watch. He kneels beside us and he puts a hand on both of our knees and he lets out a gasp and then stands up so I think he will leave. He yells so loud in his hands over the water.

"We need an evac now."

And I think it's weird that his knees are hairy like his lips. He has a walkie-talkie in his hand he is yelling and crying and I don't know why and really big boots. He doesn't look like a policeman or even one who isn't a policeman and I close my eyes because I'm tired so I just hang onto Stick. The man lifts my head and he puts water in my mouth and I open my eyes again. There is no white van. I see he has put his shirt over Stick. There is a piece of chocolate in my mouth so maybe puppies next. I want to run but if this is the stranger's candy I guess I will have to eat it and I will get dead.

"Anna?" he says and he smiles a nice smile. "My name is John."

Even though the mustache and his hands are strong I put my head back and stop the worry worms because the chocolate is there in my mouth and all melty.

I hear more people and there are all sorts of bossy and yelling and I keep my eyes shut so no one bosses me. I feel my body lift up and I jerk my head and look up. And then I bend my arm and she is not there. No brown fur and I need a sniff but she is gone.

"Gwen?"

"Who's Gwen?" a woman says. There are very many people and they all stop and look at me. I feel like I am the chocolate chip in the cookie.

"The bear," I say.

"Oh, Jesus." The woman puts her hand on her mouth. "She must have seen the whole thing."

"Not Jesus," I say. "My lost teddy, Gwen."

Part III

Pembroke Hospital
and Toronto, 1991

26.

I don't want to open my eyes and there is Jessica's hamster in my mouth. The hamster is called Fluffy and she came to kindergarten with Jessica last year. The first day she just sat in a corner and didn't move and I think she was really dead but I didn't say because it would make Jessica sad and make her cry because she didn't want a hamster she wanted a dog but she was only allowed a hamster instead. Fluffy was white with a bit of black in some places but when we first met I didn't know about the black because mostly it was underneath. There was a tiny body but she looked bigger because her hair stands up and sticks right out from her body like at the science center when I went and the man in the white coat picked me and I stood at the front. Everyone watched and my hand went on a big silver ball and that made my hair go on end but I didn't know. Everyone was laughing and I was too because my tummy was not happy and I wasn't sure if I'd barf and then the man in the white coat held up a mirror so I could see my hair all stuck straight up on my head. Like Fluffy.

But it wasn't until a little while after Fluffy moved into our class that I got to hold her and have a talk. When I did hold her she was lighter than I could believe and had little pink toes and I saw claws but they didn't hurt even though they were a little scratchy. I gave her a piece of carrot and she went chew chew chew but really fast and holding the carrot her hands almost looked like hands. I was surprised that her body was so small inside the fur and I put my cheek on her and it felt tickly but also so so soft and I tried to give her a kiss. I had to sink my lips really far into Fluffy's fur to find her body so she would know it was a kiss and then some fur got in my mouth and blech I breathed it in too much. The teacher told me to stop scaring the hamster. I had to put her back and hang my tongue out of my mouth and Jessica helped me pick off the fluffies from Fluffy and they were nice and soft out of my mouth but not in.

And it feels like there are all these fluffies in my mouth except not her little body or hands that look like hands and I'm glad about that. I try to open my eyes and someone has stuck glue in my eyelashes to make them shut. Maybe I am supposed to sleep and I am naughty and wouldn't and so that is the punishment gluing eyes except I know it isn't. I get my one eye to open just a little crack and it looks white. My stomach goes whoop doop and I remember the forest and the trees and the lake but the white isn't there. I look through the crack again and there is no blue or green or brown and there is no windy or rain pouring on my head and I think that is good and close my eye crack.

I hear eeeeeee and I think uh-oh bugs and maybe mosquitoes but they don't sound the same. The buzzy fly keeps buzzing and

I am being bent at the waist and I think that is weird because it's like my head is lifting to the sky with my body too but I am not pushing it there. I would like to smack the fly but my arm has no blood left inside or maybe the bone is gone so now I just have a floppy arm that dangles like Stick's dingle or like an elastic that is wider and might be on newspaper that you can collect to make a ball that bounces like a real ball if you do it for years and years. The buzzy fly stops so I think phew I don't have to worry about smacking it with no swatter or my hand or if I had a shoe but I left them somewhere and I don't know where. There is no buzzy fly and my body is sitting up.

"Anna?"

I open my eye crack to look. It is very white all over and I think maybe the moon. A lady that is a stranger is talking in a singsong to try and sound like Momma but she is older and not the same sniff. My eye crack shuts.

"Drink."

There is something on my lips and they are wet and I think oh no Fluffy will drown but a little piece of water slides into my mouth and Fluffy is not there it is only like the fur that got left behind and Jessica forgot some or it stuck to her fingers and got back inside. A bit more pieces of water and the fluffs get pushed down and they don't taste as much anymore and that is a little bit better.

"Good girl."

The lady is in my eye crack and she smiles. "How are you feeling?"

I don't know.

"You need to eat something."

The lady turns away and her sniff goes with her and then it

comes back again like a cookie that is not chocolate or a blah Arrowroot but has white powdery things on top. I don't really think this is my favorite cookie but okay. She is holding something and she pulls a table that goes across my body and there is a bowl that has a little metal hat. I didn't know that a bowl could have a hat and this one does and is that because it gets cold sometimes or why? I want to know and I open my mouth and Fluffy is gone but a big frog has jumped in. That's what Momma says it is and this frog has claws not just toes and he has scratched my throat because he wanted to get out or he was stuck behind Fluffy and there was a lineup.

"It's okay." The lady puts a sugar hand on me and her lips are so red. "You don't need to talk."

And I don't but that doesn't say why a bowl has a hat but she takes the hat off and sitting there is ice.

"You are in the hospital."

It is not the moon but it is very white. "Hospital" is a hard word to say because I tried a long time ago when Grandma was sick and it came out like "hospickle" and everyone laughed and that was before I got rid of my brain worms that are gone now. There is orange ice that looks like that juice that is called Tang that we are allowed sometimes only in summer as a treat. Except it is in an ice cube from the freezer and maybe more like a Popsicle?

"You were very, very thirsty. That's why your throat hurts."

So she doesn't know about the frog and I don't tell her because there is a good time for secrets and I don't want people to take Fluffy or the frog and they might because they don't say you just come to school one day and Fluffy is gone and there is no cage and no morning soft snuggle with no kiss.

The lady puts a spoon in the bowl and captures the Tang ice cube and I watch it and she starts to put it close to my mouth. It goes wiggle wiggle wiggle on the spoon and my eyes are wide because it is really funny except I can't quite laugh because my head hurts but I wish Stick could see. I was supposed to bring Stick to the moon and I didn't. I don't know where Stick is and maybe lost. If Stick watched the ice cube wiggle on the spoon he would giggle and that makes me giggle and then he giggles and I giggle and then we both get the flops because we are so giggly. I miss Sticky. So I think the wiggle is funny but I can't laugh because no Stick so I just look at it and the lady is bringing it closer to me and even more closer and I don't know why so I look at her.

"Funny." I smile.

She smiles big on her face. "You like it?"

I don't know what she means so I look back at the Tang ice cube. She keeps putting the spoon at me and then has it so close to my face I can't watch it wiggle anymore. She pushes the spoon on my lips. I can't see because my nose is in the way and I feel cold on my lips. I got an ice cube from the freezer because I like them and I play with them until they are gone but I'm not supposed to because I forgot and then there is a puddle that I get in trouble about. I sneaked one from the freezer with a chair but Momma saw the chair and knew and so I tried to stick the ice cube in my mouth to hide it and it got stuck to my tongue. Momma said don't pull it off so I had to sit with it and my tongue went into the ice and Momma poured water on my tongue and it came off. The lady doesn't have water and I don't want my tongue to be captured by ice.

I close my lips together.

"You don't like Jell-O?" says the lady. "Try. It's good to get something in your stomach."

"Jell-O?"

"Yes. Orange."

Oh. I really want Jell-O and I am never even allowed it before. If Momma pushes the door and gives me a kiss she will see me and maybe Daddy but he doesn't care about candy as much so okay. I open my mouth and she turns the spoon and it goes plop and there is a little bit of Tang but then it goes wiggle wiggle and oh yuck that's weird and my tongue says no thanks and tssssuffff I spit. The ice cube wiggles out of my mouth and goes through the air and over the bowl and the bowl's hat and lands on the tray behind those.

"Nice shot," says the lady.

I nod and I am proud and I spit pretty far but I am really tired.

27.

"Someone is here to see you," the lady singsongs through my eye cracks.

I open them and the room is so white and not the moon then Grandpa in the door. I smile because I love Grandpa and he smells like pipe and is really nice. He comes to the bed and he puts his big hand on me that is always scratchy and fingernails that are thick and Daddy says he must need a saw to cut them. Grandpa's face is looking at me and he has a sort of smile and a sort of not smile.

"Hi," I say.

He leans in and hugs me and I get to smell pipe and maybe a little of what Momma uses to clean the bathtub when we do it together on a sponge and it is yellow or like green and thick to make the bathtub white again. Grandpa doesn't say hi back and that is like always because he says it with his eyes. I can hear him through his eyes so he doesn't need to speak English like Stick doesn't and no brain worms just his eyes. He is on a chair and sits by my bed and has a hand on my arm. I must be his favorite because I'm getting all the attention. He smiles more and then has something behind his back and I know that his eyes say to me that it is present time and not even Christmas or a birthday I don't think because Momma would have a calendar with Xs so I know. He pulls out his arm and stuck on the end of it is Gwen!

Grandpa puts Gwen on my face and I hug her so tight and sniff and she has too much like something wrong is inside her and smelly soap but I don't care because I can hug it out of her long enough so she will smell just right. She puts her stitched mouth against my cheek and she really really missed me. We love each other and we hug for a long time and I am so happy I have a big smile.

"Thank you," I say to Grandpa because manners.

He nods and he is smiling in his eyes and I see they are a little red like he was in the pool but no goggles and I've never seen Grandpa goggles. I would like to go swimming in the pool but I am too tired and not now because Gwen doesn't go swimming. I don't want to leave her in bed like normal so I don't ask to go to the pool. I want to just stay with Gwen.

"That warden, John, went back for her," says Grandpa.

I think he means to the pool.

Another lady comes in with no Jell-O and she makes a big smile and has crayons. Her smile has really red lips and I think that she drew it on with one of her crayons. She puts the crayons on my tray and I have a piece of paper too. I want to make a paper hat for Grandpa but she says it is time to draw pictures. She asks me what I want to draw and I say Gwen. I draw a teddy that is not swimming and it looks like Gwen with brown fur and a black nose and the lady says would I like to draw something else? I say I would like to finish Gwen and she says what about from my trip. I say no thank you because manners and Grandpa gives me a twinkle smile. The lady and her crayon mouth smile more and I wonder if she left any red.

"Did you see your mother, Anna?" She asks me and I nod yes.

"A bit soon," Grandpa says to the lady. He is standing on his feet and his big hand is on my shoulder and it feels nice and heavy but he looks at the lady not me.

"It's a first assessment."

And I don't know that and Grandpa says "Harrumph" and sits down. His hand isn't on my shoulder anymore but I feel his finger on mine and he has a leather hand. The lady asks me what she looked like and I think I'm not sure when. The lady says when I was on the island and not that long ago and I miss my momma and wish she would come. And the lady says in the trees when Stick and I were alone and did I see Momma? The crayon smile goes wide and she asks me to draw a picture and so I don't know what she wants. I put a circle on the paper to start and she says "Oh, that's the island" and I nod okay and she means when Stick and I were lost and I worry that Stick is gone. I lost him or maybe Momma and Daddy know that they left me behind. There are many things and they make me feel worry. She asks what else there was and so I put a tree because I saw him and there were trees when he was lost. I found him again and I think I should tell her. She wants me to draw so I make the trees and I put Stick's body in them in the middle like how maybe he got lost. I can't remember when I saw him the last time before.

"That's her," says the lady.

I had more colors because Stick needs yellow fluffy hair or

you don't know it is Stick. And I put pants but then I forgot no pants so I try to rub out the pants except I use black to make it look like the dirt on him. I put green plants in the dirt so everyone can tell it is dirt because the roots of the plants are stuck into it to grow. The black doesn't look rubbed but it does look like dirt.

"Like an angel in the trees," says the lady.

I say I don't know and Grandpa's eyebrows wiggle so wrong answer so I say yes with my head nod. And the lady asks why the skin is all white and I wonder if she's ever seen Sticky's hair because it is like that really yellow and it's not the skin. The lady says it looks like the person in my picture has swallowed the moon because of the skin and I am feeling tired and I don't really want to do pictures anymore. The lady asks if I want to put any more in and I look at her mouth moving with cracks in her lips. I try to get the red.

"Good choice." She hands me the red.

There is a lot of red left and surprise because so much is on the lady's mouth and I wish she would go away so I want to take her red. I put it in my fist like a baby holds a crayon and I start to press hard and make the paper as red as I can and all over the place. I look at it and ha-ha because now Stick is stuck in the picture and it looks like he has the lady's lips all over him. I don't like the lady and I hope she feels sad because I used her red and I look at her to see. She is looking at the picture and she has one hand on her chest and one on her mouth and she says, "Oh, we'll need to work that through."

That lady and her crayons leave and Grandpa says "Good."

He stays for a long time and I like him sitting by me and the singsong lady brings a tray. Everyone on the tray has a hat and she takes off the hats and there is soup and a little sandwich with no crusts yay. I take a bite of the little sandwich because I like triangles and the points taste the best. I eat all three points and that leaves me with the circle middle and so I can pop that in my mouth and then the next and I gobble it all down and the soup that Grandpa helps me. It slides on my chin and there is a cookie that the lady gives to my hand and it is a little bleh like Arrowroots but it is okay. And my body feels better because of the cookie and my toes twinkle and say thank you and so I feel better and I would like to see Momma.

I look at Grandpa's face and I feel worried about asking because his eyes say no but I need to see Momma because she needs to know that Gwen is back because she will be very worried.

"Did you see it?" Grandpa says in a very little voice.

"See what?"

"The bear."

Grandpa's face looks twisty and I see water in his eyes and I feel like he is looking inside me. I know it will be safer if he knows I am different and I shake my head. I point to my belly. "I have the black dog."

"Bear?"

And I don't know what Grandpa is saying and he has a cry coming from his eye and I feel sad because I didn't know a grandpa could cry. I want him to be okay again.

"Yes." I pat my tummy. "Black dog bear."

It makes Grandpa happy and I am a good girl. He gives me a big hug and he is warm. I want everyone to be like usual and nice and I give him a kiss.

"Momma?"

Grandpa doesn't say anything and he takes a nose breath like

Stick except his nose is like five noses the size of Sticky's so it is a louder and big breath. There is still air for me because they have lots in a hospital but if I was somewhere with less air like a tent I think I couldn't breathe very good because the biggest noses like Grandpa would suck it all in and none left for me. And maybe there isn't quite enough in the hospital because I try and suck in through my mouth and my nose but it's still not in my body so I hope Grandpa stops breathing quite so much or the other adults with big noses.

"Your mother is not with us."

I nod and there is a window on the other side of the room that I didn't know and I wonder where we left her. And a TV and I would like to watch cartoons.

"Do you understand?" asks Grandpa.

I nod again because I am listening and that is manners.

"She's in heaven now."

"When will she visit me?"

"She's staying there. She'll be waiting."

So much waiting all the time. My grandpa puts his chin on his chest and I know that Momma said this to me and so that is true but Grandma is dead too and in the hospital is when she died so I am dying too and the too-wiggly Jell-O was how I know there is bad things.

"I am dead?"

"No." My grandpa lifts his head and looks at me and his eyes are red more now and he didn't go in the pool and I see a small leak and so I know he is crying because how much he misses Grandma and me too so I get a tear in my eye because I would like her to come and visit me too in the hospital if I'm going to die and then I won't see her.

"When will I die?"

"Not for a long time."

And I sigh because that sounds so long it is boring and Stick must be waiting dead too. So it is just Grandpa and Gwen and me in the whole wide world and I hope not more Jell-O.

But it is too bad if Stick is dead because then I can't teach him to spit Jell-O. I miss Stick so much and I feel my eyelids pull down hard. He could try and spit Jell-O and I would really spit it and if the lady or Grandpa got us caught I could say it was Stick and they would believe me because the Jell-O would smoosh on his face and wiggle there. And also Stick would laugh at the Jell-O and I could make it wiggle a lot so he keeps laughing and I want him to know about Jell-O.

"Can Sticky see?"

"Who?"

"Stick."

"You need a stick for something?"

"Alex."

"Your brother?"

"Can he see?"

"Not when his eyes are closed."

"Because he got dead."

"No. He's asleep."

"In heaven?"

My grandpa's two hairy eyebrows are trying to get tied up in the middle of his face. "He's right there," he says and points.

I turn my head and look and there is a bed and this stumpy body and it's Stick! I didn't know he was there and I know most times because of his loud nose breath. No fair because he is close to the TV and that doesn't mean he gets to pick the shows because those will be boring and baby and I am better at picking. But he is lying there and a sheet on his body but little arms are sticking out and he got a needle in one hand. Ouch. Except his face is gross. The tomato is really red and gooey and like a tomato got rotten and dropped on the ground and I think ugh. Bigger than even before. And I feel sorry for Sticky having that face but did he see my Jell-O that went far when it spit? So I want to ask him. I look and in the squish of the tomato I think his eyes are shut and I guess that's why the lady gives me Jell-O and not him. I worry that I wasn't looking through my eye cracks and he snuck cookies. I will keep watching because I want cookies too and that's not fair if the lady just gives them to Stick.

"Poison ivy," Grandpa says.

"Yuck."

"Yeah." Grandpa does a very small laugh that I can barely hear. "I'll say."

I stare at Stick because I can wake him up like that and not get in trouble most days because I didn't do anything. I can't do it now because the poison is shutting his eyes. I look at his big smooshed head and I feel my heart when I lost him and it makes me want to cry. I sniff Gwen and hug and I want to watch TV and so I stare at it and hope it will turn on. It is so close to Stick's bed that I bet if I had that bed I could crawl to the bottom and be close enough to reach it and not fair because Stick is sleeping and too puffy to see anyway.

"Don't worry; he's going to be fine," I hear Grandpa say.

I stare at the TV more because maybe it is a hint and he will see with his eyes that I want it on.

"You took care of him."

I nod because manners and keep looking at the TV.

"My girl." Grandpa touches my arm. "You did real good."

"Okay." I feel tired and so does Gwen.

"How 'bout a little TV?" says Grandpa.

And I smile.

28.

Grandpa is in his chair. Our house is dark and smells like pipe because it is nighttime. I am in my pj's and on the top stair and it looks funny because the chair is in the front window of our house and not his house. I don't know how the chair walked all the way from his house because it has no legs and it is here forever now. Only four small wood feet. Grandpa is asleep in the chair. I think the chair started to float in the wind and it got picked up and flew out the window at his house and down the street even though I know it didn't. The wind blew harder and Grandpa went up into the sky and the cloud bounced and it wasn't a rainy one so his socks didn't get wet and he kept asleep and floated.

My feet are cold and I go creak creak creak down the stairs because our house is old. The stairs always tell on me. I had a cold in the hospital. It is better and Rose the housekeeper after Grandma died came from Grandpa's house to our house. She found cream for skin that smelled not right and she put so much on I had a mustache. Stick laughed at my mustache and I didn't think it was funny until I looked in the mirror and saw. I laughed and even I didn't feel like it. Rose laughed and then she took the scrubber and cleaned the toilet. I don't have a cold anymore and Grandpa is resting his old bones in his chair.

Our house is different now. Grandpa's chair sits in our house and Rose opens the door all day. I don't need school. Sticky's hair gets brushed every morning and he doesn't know why. People at the door have food. Or the door opens and I don't know the people and I am supposed to smile but it's okay if I don't feel like it. I just woke up and it was nighttime and I thought I was in the hospital or on the moon but I am not. I am at our house but it doesn't feel like our house. Grandpa is at our house all the time not just special days and that is nice.

I woke up and I called out for Momma but only in my head. It is nighttime and dark. She didn't come and that's how I knew that I am living inside of my dream. If I am having a bad dream she says I should get up and pee. The bathroom light is on. I remember the tent. The most important thing is I have to re-member to pee after I get to the toilet. There is no toilet when we are camping. There is a toilet in my house and I peed and still Momma didn't come so I have to be inside my dream.

I creak on the stairs and it doesn't even wake Grandpa up. If Daddy was sleeping on the couch he would wake up and smile with warm whiskers. Grandpa has a little snore and very white hair that looks like Rumpelstiltskin made it on a spinner and put silver on his head in a very nice way. His skin is brown and wiggly like Daddy's shoe that is leather but on Grandpa's cheek except he has gray eyes that are from Momma's and mine and

Stick's. I like his little snore and his chest goes up and down. I touch his knee.

"Wha?"

Grandpa's head lifts up like a turtle out of his shell. There was a turtle at school except his name might have been Francis or Franny and I can't remember. He had crinkles on his neck. The turtle poked his head out and blinked his eyes at me and that's how we became friends except not as much friends as Fluffy the hamster but still a lot. Grandpa's eyes open and they look more like water in a pool and there is a new part of red around the sides. I reach up and say ouch to his eyes.

"Red, huh?" He sniffs his nose.

I sniff my nose too.

The toadstool of Grandpa's chair is stuck out from the bottom and I put my knee on it to climb up and it goes thump and shuts. I go whump. My bum goes bang on the floor.

"Whoa!" Grandpa kicks forward and pulls me up on his lap. I am safe and he reaches down to the magic handle at the side of the chair and makes the toadstool pop back out. We go leaning back and his feet go up in the air on the toadstool at the same time. If the wind comes we will float down the street and that's in my dream too.

"Still not talking, Anna?"

I cuddle my face into his soft shirt and he smells nice like Daddy's leather shoe too. Not a turtle.

"That's okay." He pats my head. "What time is it? Still time to sleep."

I put my ear on Grandpa's chest and listen to rumble.

"Had a bit of trouble myself."

I listen and da-thump. His voice sounds like bark is stuck

in his throat and it is making him whisper. He goes ahem and it rumbles. It is like very quiet thunder boom boom swish and rumble rumble. His arms squeeze. I blink. We stay in Grandpa's chair and my head on his chest and it goes up and down. I let my eyes fall and my head feels lighter and finally because a cloud comes by and I think that is nice.

"I miss her so much," he says.

29.

I hear Rose is calling me and Gwen doesn't answer. I am put back in bed and someone lifted me here not Daddy. I pull the blanket up to my chin and even though the sun is outside. Gwen is cold. I am in my room and it is my favorite place but maybe not so much now I am older. It is light blue like the sky and because Momma said that went with a part of my eyes. I used to lie in bed and feel like I am floating in the sky. I like my room and I like my bed and I feel worried so I can't float. I sniff Gwen. I don't feel like I am floating anymore even though the room is blue. My head is heavy and it won't let me go up.

I roll on my back and Gwen tucks under my chin and I can see the tree is waving its leaves at me. I say a hello but only in my head. If it's in a dream I can't talk out loud. In a dream my voice doesn't really come out of your mouth. Even once Daddy said I was shouting out my dream but he said that is because I was waking up and so the dream went across from where I sleep to where I really awake. When the dream goes across I will wake up. When I yell in my sleep Daddy needs to come and climb into my bed for a snuggle. I will wake up. That's when my voice will come out loud from my mouth.

"Anna?"

Rose says my name and she doesn't say Gwen's so Gwen doesn't know that she is being called. She just stays tucked in and wants me to stay there too. I pull the blanket up and it is a bit darker except not that dark. Rose's head comes into my room. "There you are, dear. Gave me a fright. I didn't see you under the blanket."

Gwen says oh.

"You'll come down now? There's someone...well, I made cookies."

Gwen pokes me with a round, fuzzy hand.

"Come before the cookies all disappear down your brother's throat."

The blanket comes away from my head and it is daytime again. Rose has a fold on her face that goes into a smile and her hand on my forehead and feels like cool butter that comes out of the fridge.

"Come, sweet thing." She pulls us up to sit and gives me a sugar hug. I like Rose.

Rose and I tuck Gwen into the blanket with her head on the pillow. Gwen is still cold. I hold Rose's butter hand and my feet are on the stairs and creak creak and the smell of cookies and Stick is running around with two cookies. He wouldn't be allowed by Momma for breakfast except Rose gave him two.

"Nana-nanananana," he yells when he sees me and he has the

cookie crazies from so much. I hear a stranger voice and I look. Sitting on the couch is the lady with the crayon smile. My stomach thinks oh no. The crayon drawing on her lips spreads out and she has her eyes on me. It means I am her person. I don't want her back.

I want to sniff Gwen. I turn to go back upstairs to get her. Grandpa is there and takes my hand. Rose puts a cookie in my other hand and I look up at her with sad eyes like Stick does. Stick is not that smart but sometimes he has a point and she puts another cookie in my hand. I say in my voice inside my head that the second cookie is for Gwen and that I am not a piggy like Sticky. He is running around and laughing and Grandpa says for him to come. Grandpa has a ball and they go into the backyard. I watch because that's where maybe I would like to go. Nobody asks me to be there too.

Rose puts a glass of milk on the coffee table with a coaster underneath because she says the wet rings on wood are her trouble now. She tells the crayon lady that she gets used to cleaning with kids and puts mayonnaise on the rings on the table. Then it takes the rings away and that is better. I look at the table and I see the rings that happened when Stick left his sippy cup for a really long time and Momma forgot. I want it to stay with no mayonnaise. I put my hand on the ring. The crayon lady looks at me and says "It's okay, Anna." Rose gives me another cookie and then she is gone and I feel bad and she left maybe because I said no mayonnaise on the table. Now it is only the crayon lady. She smells like crackers.

The crayon lady has her crayons because she always does. And a piece of paper. She puts a paper in front of me and I nibble a cookie. My front teeth are like Fluffy and they chew chew fast and get a chocolate chip out. I look for another chocolate chip and there are lots because Rose puts in lots.

"Would you like to talk?"

I nibble nibble.

"Would you like to draw?"

I look at the crayon lady and her lips are so red and I see the red in her crayon box is used a lot. I put my shoulders up and she puts a crayon in my hand. It is blue so she thinks I am a boy. She doesn't know. I put it down and look for a better one.

"I had a nice talk with your brother."

I look up at the crayon lady and wonder if she gave him a Popsicle to get him to talk. I know Stick doesn't speak that many words. One of his tricks is sad eyes and maybe a giggle and he gets treats. I look at the table and I see that there is yogurt in a bowl and all messy so the crayon lady got him to talk because he sits in one place for long enough to get food in his mouth only. The yogurt is blue so blueberry. A spoon is sitting in the bowl. The wrong end sticks out and yogurt is finger-painted on the spoon hand. That means Stick's sticky hands.

"He told me your father is at work."

I stare at the spoon and I can hear Stick saying "werk." I knew that he needs something to eat yogurt with. I speak Sticky's language and the crayon lady doesn't. I smile a little and Stick is funny.

"Do you know where your father has gone?"

I look at the crayon lady and I don't know what the answer is that will make her know she can go away. I think manners so I just smile a little. I don't really think smile. She maybe sees that my eyes don't think smile because she puts the crayon lips together and pushes the box toward me. I forgot that I am picking a color. I don't know what to draw. Maybe I want yogurt but not really and I could draw our house or our family and that's what school always wants. Something else is better and maybe a balloon. I see the red crayon and it is stubby and the paper had to be peeled back. The lady uses too much of it for her lips. Momma would say share but I don't want the lady's red crayon because she has touched it.

"Do you know what it means when someone dies?"

Momma likes canoes better than loud boats. She likes Algonquin Park because most people aren't there now and it will be only our family. We will be all together because we are so big and we will fill up all the empty space. And that's how I think of our family when I draw us for school. Daddy's and Momma's legs are really long and stretch up for most of the whole paper. I am long too and I have on my pink socks that can even go over my knee when I really pull. Stick is a little stumpy thing and not big except his head because it is. But the whole picture uses lots of color and is big enough to be from side to side and we make it so full.

"It is not like sleep. It means that life stops. When people die they do not come back."

The crayon lady can hear my inside thoughts and maybe that is because I am dreaming. I wonder if she can see my brain worms and I feel mad. And there is one crayon that is brown and it still has a tip that is perfect and she hasn't touched it. I know what crayons look like when they just come out of a box. No one really likes brown and same with me. The brown has no paper peels and I think Gwen is like that brown. She is upstairs warm and sleeping. I am happy when I think about Gwen so I take the brown.

"Do you have anything you would like to ask me, Anna?"

I left Gwen upstairs and mistake. I want to go and get her. I am stuck with the crayon lady and manners. I draw Gwen and I do sometimes when I was at school too. I miss her. Her ears are circles and except they don't have a bottom part on the circle and I do her little round head with the black stitches that are her little bit of smile. I need the black and I make them black. I do her body and it has lighter patch of fur that is a little soft and so I make the hairs show that sometimes tickle my nose. She has stubby legs and arms and beans somewhere in her bum. I don't put those in because they are inside her body and the stitches keep them in. I can't see them but I can feel them when I squish.

"A bear?"

I draw on her fur and keep the little hairs small because they are more like a carpet than Stick's head. So so soft. I put in the stitches that are claws. Even though the black crayon is a bit more used that is okay because I need it only for a little bit. I make the best picture of Gwen ever. I want to show it to Momma so much. My tummy feels empty because I want to get Gwen. I miss her and would like to sniff.

"That's a good girl, Anna."

I wonder if my drawing is so good that it sniffs and I hold it to my face and take a big sniff. And no. It smells like crayon but okay because it is so nice. It has a warmer smell like on the dock at our cottage. I feel cold. Crayons and the dock are nice. Sometimes I lie on the dock because my skin and hair is wet. The warm wood melts into my bones. I think my bones are like metal. Once the wood heats up enough it makes my bones warm. My bones push the hot around to everywhere in my body. A towel comes over me and I keep my eyes shut really tight and only look at the orange inside my eyes. It is orange and the sun made a dot that looked more like the moon and if I squished it goes brighter red. When I open the sun smiles right inside my eyes and I have to squint and whisper thank you because it keeps heating me. I want Momma.

"We'll make our peace with that bear."

I need a fire inside my bones.

30.

The doorbell rings and Rose goes to the door again. I think something in a pretty dish that smells like cheese and bread will come inside. Or maybe it is lucky and a chocolate cake. Grandpa points his eyes at me and I know but I am stuck and have to say hello. I sit on the stair. I look at Grandpa and the door opens more and Rose steps away and points her eyes at me. It is a parent in the door.

Grandpa says ahem. "Anna, say hello to Mr. . . ."

I smile a little at the parent because manners but I am used to seeing him. It is Steven and Grandpa doesn't know because Momma does playdates. I hear Steven's feet step forward.

I don't feel like saying hello to Steven and so he says that is okay sometimes. I look at his feet and then I see a small black shiny foot. A girl steps out for a second. I watch the pink shine float around her legs like it is barely touching. It is Jessica. Her bangs are extra straight and round. I think the big brush that has pig wires might be stuck in the front of her head because they are so bouncy and smooth. Only just the bangs are like that. She has a pink dress with a skirt that stands out. It is shiny and at the bottom there is a crinkly bit. That means it stands out all by itself with no wind blowing.

I hear Jessica say my name and I don't say anything. The shiny pink and then socks that turn over like white Kleenexes. A hand goes down on her back and she pushes forward from the leg and looks shy like it is picture day. Except I don't think yes because that is at school and she is at my house. She has hands behind her back and looks at the ground. Pink cheeks and a hand does a tap tap and she says "Hi, Anna" and looks at Steven.

I stay sitting on the stairs. My hand is on my bangs. They don't hang down or go smooth. I think that I was in the canoe and I had wet bangs. A bear walked on the beach and his nose was in the air. He was sniffing up with his nose and scared off Snoopy and even the black dog. There was no brush or a hair dryer to push hot hair and even no plug. Jessica doesn't know. Momma only has a comb and I said it's a brush and it is round. Momma has one that is more like a square. She tries and my bangs go straight and not round. Not smooth but little parts that fly up. And I say that it's too fluffy. I don't want to look like Fluffy because that is a hamster. Not like a real lady. I stand up and stamp my foot on the stairs. They go creak creak. I feel so mad and twist my hands in my pj's and they are still on my body. No dress. And my pj top even has little teddies like a baby and there are cookie crumbs. Momma doesn't do it right. I hate Momma! I scream and it turns into a cry. Jessica walks backwards. Steven puts his head down. Rose is on the stairs and I see Grandpa waving his hand. Stick has a truck in his hand. I cry and cry and I hate them. And Rose has her sugar arms on me and rocks and says "There, there, baby." She asks me what is wrong and my inside head voice can't say. I am not a baby. I cry and I cry so hard. I feel tired and sniff. My lake is empty. And there is nothing else to cry.

But then Rose has a Popsicle not broken in half. It is pink. I get it all. And I get shooed out to the backyard and still in my pj's but I don't care until I eat the Popsicle. I see my tree and Jessica and Stick are playing with the sand. They always do when we have playdates with Steven at our house. Momma said Jessica is like Stick's babysitter even though she is too young. Momma said it keeps Stick from crying. Jessica fills up a bucket and she pats the sand on the top with a shovel. She turns the bucket over very fast. There is a castle except flat on the top no point or princess in the top tower. Stick brings his fists down and smashes. He laughs and laughs until he rolls on his bum. He thinks it is so funny. Jessica isn't mad. She smiles and she laughs at Stick like he is funny. She starts digging the shovel in to the sand to fill up the bucket again.

I don't want to play that game. The sun is on the grass and it is melting my Popsicle. The sun has an invisible tongue that likes to lick my Popsicle. It licks the good part when it gets runny on the side. I walk to the back of the grass and my Popsicle drips a bit on the ground. My tree wants a drip so I walk over and lean the stick at the bottom and drip drip drip. It gets three drips and then the rest for me.

"Oh, Anna, is that you?"

The fence is talking. I didn't know it knows my name. That is kind of funny so I laugh and then a head comes over the top. It is white and has curls that sometimes hold pins in them. It is Mrs. Buchanan and her jeans are rolled up to show ankles. "I heard you were back, but I haven't wanted to bother you. All those newspapermen after you?"

And I look behind me and there are no newspapers. Maybe she puts them down for Snoopy. When he was a baby she said to stop his poop on the carpet. I don't know why there are newspapers and Mrs. Buchanan keeps talking about them and like they are in our house. And then my heart goes whoa and I put my hand on the spot. Mrs. Buchanan knows. She can see that I am different because the black dog is inside.

I see the back gate open. Stick looks up with a funny face. Jessica pulls him back to pay all his attention to her. Stick peeks at the gate and sees Mrs. Buchanan is there and Sticky starts to cry. Jessica makes a cooing over him and stands him on his legs. She brushes the sand from his bum. She takes his hand and tells him to go inside and now he is her best friend. Not me.

"I'll let Snoopy in," says Mrs. Buchanan. "He wants to see you."

Snoopy runs at me and he comes up fast and stops just before me and doesn't push. I feel a big smile because I love Snoopy. We love each other so much. Snoopy rubs on me and gives me a big kiss on the lips. His tongue goes up my nose and I laugh. He is licking my Popsicle and I say "Hey" and pull it away. He stops licking but stares at it with both eyes and hangs his tongue out really long. He keeps staring and tail wagging because he really really wants it so much. I take more licks and I am glad that Snoopy is with me. I give him more licks of my Popsicle and even break off a part. I pinch it between two fingers. He takes it from my fingers and I feel his teeth are gentle on my fingers. They touch but they don't bite or scrape or smell bad. I know that is not what I saw. I ask him with my eyes if he saw Coleman when I was inside. He says no and wag wag wag. I say I knew it wasn't you.

Snoopy licks my face. I pat his black hair and I point to my chest and show him why we are best friends. I was away and a black dog jumped in me. He wags and I say that's why Mrs. Buchanan will give us both newspapers. Now we are the same. We rub on each other and I wag too. And we touch our noses and I feel so happy. We are the same now and can be in the yard and play and I get a ball and we run and run. And then I am tired and so is Snoopy. We lie down under the tree. I put my head on Snoopy's belly and look up at the branches that wave in the sky.

I open my eyes in a second but it must be later and Snoopy is not under my head. I wipe my eye and think I have a paw but no. I have a hand like a girl. Except that if I could see inside with X-ray eyes I know that I am different from everybody. Grandpa's knees are standing in front of my eyes. I hear him saying did I fall asleep? I don't know and he sits on the ground beside me and puts his back on the tree. He moves my head onto his leg and I look up and so I see up his nose and hairs. I watch his face crumple up a bit like a sponge when it is dry and crinkles and should have more water. Except if you put water on it it would get soft and spongier and Grandpa's face isn't. I wonder if his face will crack and I get a little worry. Then I think that sponges don't break so it will be okay. Grandpa is talking in a sad voice and how dreams come in the day but I don't know all the words. He puts his hand on my back and hangs his head down too like Snoopy when a dog is bad.

31.

Rose puts macaroni and cheese in my bowl for dinner. It isn't the right kind so I know it is still a dream day because it is white and not orange and the noodles are big and curled and I want them straight and skinny. Rose says it's from scratch. I didn't scratch Stick but she says yes she knows. I want macaroni and cheese like Momma's and I tell Stick he can come to my room to play. More times I say no Stick and I put a sign on the door that says NO NO NO STICK. Except this time I want him to come.

I give Stick little Legos and he sits on his bum. He isn't good at sticking them together but I make the bottom of a castle and then he can put them onto each other to make the walls. I will be in charge of the tower because I do that the best. Soon Stick wants to leave and I have the door shut. I always shut the door to keep him out and this time he is in. I show Stick how to pull down on the handle to open the door. I have a surprise when

Stick is tall enough already. He pulls down on the handle and the door opens. He looks so happy and it's a big big smile. I say good boy and I pat his inside dog and he wags his bum and shuts the door so he can open it again. I say good boy again. He shuts the door again and he opens it again. And again. I get sick of that game so I go back to play. He keeps open shut open shut all the time.

A little thump and Grandpa stands at the door. He is watching us play and a smile is on his face. That is nice and he says he has something. His hand is behind his back and I know that is good signs. Stick takes a red Lego from me and I don't even care because of Grandpa's back. I stand up and smile. Grandpa gives Stick a red fire engine. Stick likes it because it makes the sound ba-whoo like a real one and he ignores the red block and starts rolling the truck on my bed. He doesn't say thank you and no one says "Stick, say thank you." Grandpa looks at me and I look at him and he pulls a box out from his back and it is Barbie!

I open my mouth wide. I think it is probably Jessica's when she has even more except Grandpa gives the box to me. I am not sure and he says yes and laughs and I take it and we rip it open. I worry that I am ripping Barbie's house but she tells me that she doesn't want a box house. She wants a real dollhouse and a tissue will be her sheet and a washcloth is the blanket and she needs a picture book with four corks that are the legs of her table to hold it up. I say okay. Barbie and I both know everything already. It is a really big plan. I squeeze her and the top of her head smells like a flip-flop.

I want to make her house. First I need to see her and she is so so pretty. Grandpa sits on the bed and laughs and looks at me. I say a thank-you with my eyes and he says yes he knows and puts his shoulders up. She has silver slippers that tie all the way up and real pearls are dangling down her forehead. Her tights are sparkling and I wish I had them for legs. Her skirt is poufy like cloud. The cloud is on her shoulders too.

"Jessica thought Swan Lake Barbie might be just the thing." Grandpa puts his finger on a feather and I pull Barbie away because dirt. He only laughs and his hand is on his face over his eyes. Stick is looking at the Barbie and he says "Oh, wow" because even he knows this is really really super special. Barbie and I need to have a talk and we look at each other and plan about our castles.

"Glad you like it, Anna." I see Grandpa's knees unbend and go to the door. "I never saw why she made such a big deal over a doll."

I show Barbie my jewelry box. It is the prettiest girl thing in my room and so it's a really good dream day. There is a ballerina inside that pops up on a spring and twirls to pretty music. I show Barbie and lift the lid and snap it down and the music stops and I do it again and again and it is a lid and like a mouth. When we were in Coleman and the black dog bear was chewing on the sides and making splinters. Coleman's mouth was not the same as my jewelry box but it opens and shuts the same. I click the box shut and it almost chomps my fingers. I have the smell and the red juice. The black dog is inside. He chews on my heart. I scream and I grab and he laughs. I kick and my head feels like it goes pop.

"Nana?"

I have snot and Stick is looking at me. His blue eyes are really big and his chubby cheeks are hanging on his face. I feel glad he is there. I can breathe. Then I look and he has Barbie! She is in his hand and his fingers are crushing her skirt flat. I roar and I jump and kick. He is scared and says "Waaaaah" but he won't let go of Barbie. I tackle him. He tries to run away and crying but Barbie is getting messed up and he hits her on the bed and the pearls break and go all over the room. I will never find them again. She is broken now and ruined. I make my fist into a ball and pull it back. *Thwack* into Stick as much as I can. And *pow* and his head goes back and he falls.

32.

Grandpa runs in and Stick's eye looks like it had blood on it that dripped down. Rose is gone away home at night. I am very very bad. All the love in Grandpa's heart for me is not here anymore. He says to sit in Grandpa's chair. I am not allowed to move away. He says he means it and I better not move ever. Stick has a Popsicle but not for his mouth for his eye. I stay in the chair for a long time. I have to pee. Mrs. Buchanan is there and she is staring at the eye. Grandpa won't look at me. I have to stay and I wiggle. I don't move anywhere. I feel so sick and I want to go home except I am.

I have to sit in the chair and I have to pee. No one talks to me. I don't talk and so I just sit and sit and sit. Mrs. Buchanan goes away and I think she is giving Snoopy kisses. I can hear Grandpa is putting Stick in bed. Books and more kisses and I just sit and sit forever because that's how bad I am. I think that my bowl for food will go in the backyard. Then I feel hot and not good and I pee a little. Just a little but then it all comes out even though I try to squeeze it shut. It is warm. All over the chair is wet. Grandpa's chair. I don't say and I hope no one can see. I want it to dry and it will be gone.

Grandpa comes over to the chair. He wants to take my hand but I sit on my hand. The pee is still hot and not as hot because I sat on it for a long time. My pj's are wet. I am not a baby anymore and no diapers so I am very very bad even worse. The black dog barks in me. My face is hot too. I think it is the fire that my momma and daddy sit beside and I don't want anyone to see. I look down but try not to look at the pee. It stinks. Grandpa sniffs.

"What happened here?"

I look my eyes to the side and put my arm up to cover my fire face. I am crying and I can't stop. This is Grandpa's special chair and I peed. I am bad. So now he will take it away and we will leave him too.

I feel Grandpa pull on my arm. He tugs it away from my face. I don't want to look but I don't need to because he puts my head on his shoulder. He pulls my body close to him and even if it whiffs of pee. He hugs me. He doesn't talk about anything and not about the chair. He hugs me and it helps to make the black dog lie down. He tucks his nose into his tail and that feels better. Everything is quiet now.

"Let's get you cleaned up."

Grandpa runs the bath and checks the water. He asks me to put a foot in and tell him if it is right. No bubbles but okay. He takes off my smelly pj's and tells me not to get worry about the chair. I get in the bath and the water is nice. He helps me lie back and he puts his hand under my head. I float and I feel so happy and it's what Momma and I do every time. And Grandpa starts to hum and it is the song of Momma and me. I do a big smile on my face so big it almost hits my cheeks on the sides of the tub.

"You know that tune?" Grandpa says in between his hums.

I shake my head yes.

"Ah, it's her floating song. We did this so many times."

And he keeps the humming and sings some of the words and it sounds different because his voice is sandy and shaky. I close my eyes and I can hear Momma's voice higher up and it sings with us like a ringing in the tub. I float and my hair spreads out like magic.

"Here I've been feeling sorry for what I've lost," he says. "And look at all I've got."

33.

It is nighttime again. I don't know now if it is dreaming or asleep or when the day comes. The sheet is tucked under my chin and outside the tree is waving in the moon. The lights are on outside my door. I can hear no people in the downstairs. I did hear a rumble like Grandpa's voice and now it is gone and so I think he is. I can't hear Rose's voice even though Rose says she follows the sun to our house and the sun is gone too. They are all gone so it is me and Stick. A good stranger might come to our house with more hot cheese in a bowl or cake again. I sniff and I don't smell cake. I sit up and there are no sounds.

"Momma?"

My voice goes out of my face and back into my ears. I can hear it out loud and it sounds more like the voice of a lady and maybe because now I have a Barbie. My voice is outside of my head for the first time in a long time.

"Momma?" I call out loud. "Daddy?" And nothing. No one comes for me. I am one.

I get out of bed and it's not so cold and I leave my pj's on because it's still nighttime. I walk on the carpet and the hairs tickle my feet. I see the bathroom light is on. Stick's door is open and closer to the stairs. A truck is in his door. I push the door more and look in and always it's Stick's bum hanging in the air. There is no bum. Stick isn't here and so I am alone like in the trees. Or Stick is up. Cookies! He has so many sorries because I punched his eye and is getting treats. I go quick down the stairs bounce bounce bounce and it is dark when I am on the stairs so I stop. My eyes can't see. Momma says to wait and I do and my eyes start to see more because they need minutes when it is dark outside.

I see there is something black in the living room and I think it is the black dog sitting beside the window and waiting to have a talk but I do squinty eyes and it is Grandpa's chair. It flew here and is staying now. And Grandpa. He is lying in the chair and mouth open with his feet on the toadstool. Daddy gets mad if I am up in the nighttime and so maybe Grandpa too. I walk super soft on the stairs and don't make the creaky one creak. Our house is old. It is dark and smells like pipe and is different now. I am awake.

I creep on my feet away from Grandpa and his chair and I won't want it to fly after me so shh. My bare feet smack smack smack to the kitchen. The floor is cold and my toes have to curl up to stay warm because of tiles. I see on the counter and there is the bigger square tin that Rose puts cookies inside and the lid is off! There is a cookie sitting on the counter like it is lost and no one to eat. I take a bite and check that there is no grown-up to see. There are crumbs all over and I think Stick's bum is not waving in bed because he is so busy stealing cookies.

Stick is not beside the cookies. He is gone away because I punched him. Momma said it wasn't my fault at the cottage and except this time I know it is. I feel crying and I want to see Stick and give his little belly a squeeze. Stick goes away because my whole family is gone. He didn't run away because his legs are quite short and stumpy. He doesn't run and more waddles. He waves his arms a lot and thinks he is running. I tell him he is just walking and waving his arms a lot. He says no he is running really really fast even though I know he isn't. He is gone because I am so so bad. I am the bad guy.

I feel my leg is going shaky shaky but I know that Snoopy is my only friend in the world besides Gwen. She doesn't talk even though I pretend that I can hear. I listen and my feet feel cold and maybe I do hear Snoopy in the backyard. I want to tell him the news that Stick left because I am so bad. I want to say hello and have a cuddle. Snoopy always wags and kisses me on the lips.

I walk on my bare feet to the back kitchen door and look outside the glass to see if Snoopy is outside. When I am inside and have to look out I need to smoosh eyes right to the glass and use my hands like cups around the sides. It is dark and my eyes have to try hard to see. I can see the gate and the tree and no Snoopy. I look through the fence and make my eyes squinty but I can't see him through the cracks even his nose isn't sticking in between them to sniff. The houses behind our house are big and the lights are big and in the windows. I want to know if people are inside talking. And they keep their voices soft so they don't wake me up because they think I am asleep still and how

Momma and Daddy were talking when I was in the tent and I peeked out. I think Momma's hair was hanging down like a tail. I close my eyes and I feel like I am in the blue tent and can hear the air going in and out of my brother's nose. I listen to the air.

I make my eyes squintier and I still hear the air going in and out. It sounds like Stick breath. The air stays in my ears so I look down. Tucked in by the door is a little yellow head. I nearly step on a leg again and I didn't see it because of the dark. I put my head closer and it's Stick. He is curled into a ball and sleeping by the door on the doormat. I give him a poke in his belly with my biggest toe. He keeps sleeping and his breath goes in and out and I see that he has a piece of cookie chocolate chip on the side of his mouth and that is kind of funny that he sneaks down to eat cookies. I think he probably sneaks all the time now and he is not so dumb as he used to be. I have to give him a really hard poke that is not a kick but still with my foot. His eyes go pop and are all fuzzy. He blinks and the balls of his eyes google all around his head and then he looks up.

"Nana?"

"Stick?"

"Nana."

"What are you doing?"

His eyes blink and blink.

"Are you running away, Stick?"

He shakes his head.

"I know and you are stealing cookies."

He looks like he thinks he is lost but it is just sleep fuzzies even though he doesn't speak enough words to say. I can see his punched eye where he got hurt now and the eye is like the jelly part in the middle of a doughnut and darker. Yuck. And I remember me and how I did it. I feel so bad that I punched him even though I love him.

I sit down beside him on the kitchen mat by the door and it is a little warmer than the floor. I give Stick a kiss on his cheek and it is spongy and soft and maybe the closest to a cloud that I know. "I'm sorry I punched you, Stick."

"Okey." He sniffs.

"You opened your bedroom door all by yourself and got out?" I ask.

He wags his head yes and looks proud because that is what I taught him. It means he is big. I tell him that Grandpa might get mad if he is not in bed. Bad Stick. Stick just looks sad.

"You got cookies?"

He smiles and puts his fat fingers over his mouth to cover it. One finger feels the chocolate that got rubbed off and he picks it and puts it into his mouth. "Yum."

"It's time to go to bed, Stick."

He wags his head no.

"It's the nighttime."

"No bed."

"Why not?"

He looks around and I think he is going to say cookie. He doesn't say cookie and he points at the door. I look and I speak Stick even though he doesn't say it out loud. I know why. He is waiting.

"Daddy," I say.

I look at the door too. It is closed. When the door is open, there is the backyard and then my tree and then the gate where Daddy comes in. He is not home from work. It stays shut and so Stick came down to see if Daddy came and fell asleep.

"It's bedtime," I whisper.

Stick still wags his head no. He wants to wait. I say shh so we don't wake up Grandpa. I don't want him mad again but I will not leave Stick alone. I cuddle in beside his little body. It is warm and I get in close. We sit beside the back door and it does not open. I can hear Stick's breath go in and out. He always falls asleep before me. I listen to the air of his nose. I can hear my parents' voices like at the fire but they are only in my head. Now I am awake. I know that I will wait for my parents beside Stick. And we will be waiting for a long time maybe always forever.

Epilogue

Algonquin Park, 2011

34.

I can hear my brother breathing. I step out of the canoe and look to the island. In the slanted August sun, it is just as I remember—a mat of needles on the ground, the warm scent of pine, and the sound of a lake licking the rocks. There are worn patches where tents have stood. Inside a ring of stones, the fire pit holds the remains of a burned marshmallow. I expect them to be sitting there, waiting.

"Alex?"

This was his idea. Sometime after Grandpa's funeral, he said he wanted to build a cairn for our parents on the island where they died. It must be easier for him, as he doesn't have any memories from our lost days in Algonquin Park, only the things he's learned and been told. Still, I couldn't let him come alone.

"Yeah, Anna?"

"Quit hogging all the air."

Alex reaches down, a large, veined hand, my dad's size. His

hair is cut short and streaked with white, like Mom's used to be, from a summer spent climbing in the mountains. Blond eyelashes, blue eyes; he picks up a stick, and I'm glad we are here together. I want him close. I've had the same nightmare about this island ever since I can remember. It starts when the attack is almost over. I am lying in the plants, the place where my mother must have died. The bear stands over me with a cruel look in his eyes. I know he wants me dead. I try to move, but I can't. He ducks his head to my chest. Jaws rip at my skin; they crack my bones, and he tugs the guts out of my body. He scoops my heart up into his mouth and chews. The blood drains from my veins. Soon the world goes black. I am not scared to die, but what terrifies me is that I won't be around for him. For Alex.

Alex pulls the canoe up and we walk to the clearing where our tent was pitched.

"This is where you last saw Mom?" he asks.

"No, not here," I say, looking away. "I'm not sure."

"You can't remember?"

My parents were talking. I stuck my head out of the tent and heard Mom laugh. Her ponytail hung down in a silhouette against the water. White teeth. Tanned skin. Alex was rolled up in his sleeping bag, a warm little thing with fluffy blond hair and dimpled cheeks. We were four. A family of four.

"No—I know," I say.

"Where was I?"

"Beside me, asleep in the tent."

"You remember that?"

"Yeah. You were snoring."

"I snored?"

"Some things haven't changed."

"So what did Mom say?"

"I've told you that part a hundred times."

"Tell me again."

"She lay with her arms and legs spread out like an angel. Her skin was as pale as the moon, like she had swallowed it whole. She told me to get you into the canoe."

"Was she hurt?"

"She said she loved us."

I turn away from Alex and toward the beach. The lake breathes in its bed of rock. I look out and the sky reaches out over a stand of trees on the mainland and something on the other shore catches my eye. It's a mound of grass and sticks about one hundred meters across. An old beaver dam in what must be the exact spot where our canoe landed after we paddled out.

"Remember how we were found by the warden?"

"Yeah?"

"Somewhere there." I point. "On the mainland."

"Really?"

"Yeah."

"You sure?"

"It's a beaver dam. We were found near a dam."

"I don't see it."

"Overgrown? I'm sure that's it."

"I always thought it was really far away. Just right there?"

"Just there."

Alex studies the mound. "Explains a few things."

"Like what?"

"I've always wondered: Why them and not us? We were little kids and would have been the easier prey."

"We will never know exactly why."

"That's what I mean. 'Why' is missing the point. The bear could've just swam across and got us, but he didn't."

"He spared us."

"No." He tilts his head and whispers. "He was full."

Alex breaks the long silence by wading into the shallow water and picking up a rock. He inspects it, throws it away, and picks up another. This one he keeps, and I realize he is building the cairn. The next rock he tucks into the crook of his arm. Soon he has too many to hold.

"Come help." He passes me the armful. "Where should we build it?"

I look over at the green plants. She might whisper my name.

"There?" Alex is watching me. "That's where she died?"

"Yes." I can barely say it.

"How much more haven't you told me?"

I stack the rocks. He hands me a chunk of granite. I roll it over in my hand and look for a smooth side to make sure the pyramid will be sturdy. I make a base first and then start piling rocks to get the height. One rock has a pink hue, like the blush of a cheek. Another has a white seam, a tooth. We work in silence. Soon we have a small cairn of granite and quartz. It's just a foot high, but it will hold firm through the winter. I hand a smaller rock, the size of an egg, to Alex. It has flecks of silver. He puts it in his palm and holds it tight. He uncurls his fingers and lets it catch the sun and places it on top.

I want to tell my parents everything, starting from the day I woke up in the hospital to the moment today when we pulled up to the island in the canoe. I want to tell her about my recent heartbreak, the scar on my knee, and about how I was the one who taught Alex to ride a bike. I want to tell about my night-mares, but I don't say anything. I wrap my arms around my shins and put my eyes down. My eye sockets make a perfect cup for each knee. Alex is the one who speaks.

"Mom? Dad? I love you."

I stay silent.

Finally Alex stands up. "We should get going."

I hear him scrape the canoe against the pebbles and push it out. He's right. It's time to go. The afternoon is getting on, and we don't have any camping gear. Alex sleeps out in the wild all the time, but I never do. I grab my paddle and wade in. After a second the water finds the mesh of my running shoe and seeps through. Alex is in the back of the canoe.

"Get in the front," I say.

"I'll paddle you home."

"No way. I'm your big sister. I steer."

"My turn."

"Nope."

"Fine. See ya." He uses the tip of his paddle to push the canoe away from the shore. One stroke from a long arm and the boat is moving fast, pulling something in my gut. He is leaving. I am one.

I feel the heat from the sun, the branches of the pines wave, the needles crunch underfoot, and the island tilts to make the water sway. I can smell the bear.

"You okay?" Alex says, turning back, the joke over. He gets out, pulls up the canoe, and puts a hand on my arm to steady me. "You are not okay, are you?"

"I might need a minute."

"It's my fault you came."

"Just wait?"

"Okay." He nods. "What are you going to do?"

I don't answer, because I don't know. He reluctantly gets back into the canoe. He dips the long paddle in and sculls his paddle to keep the boat in place.

I walk to the cairn and the spot in the plants where I last saw my mom. It's where all my nightmares take place. I lie down and put my foot to the edge of the rise, just like hers was. It feels as though I'm lying in her outline. I stay perfectly still. I can see the branches from a tree nodding quietly in the breeze. The sky is a deep blue with only a small wisp of cloud making its lazy way south. I close my eyes, and I can hear the soft rustle of the branches, the water licking at the shore. A small animal scurries farther away. The afternoon sun warms me. And then it is silent.

The bear is standing over me. There is no expression in his eyes other than a vague interest in food. He tugs at my chest and pulls his head up with my heart in his mouth. I feel the beats slow. The blood drains from my veins, but he only rolls my heart around on his tongue, looking bored. He spits and it falls back into my chest. And I know that he's just a dream I made up. I remember everything as it was—the stench of bear from inside the cooler, claws raking at the metal sides; Dad's severed foot with his shoe still on the end, and the thin red veins shot through my mom's eyes. Snarls of memories rise to my chest and feel like they might devour me, but then I hear a hollow thump.

My eyes pop open, and I slide them to look to the side. I am awake. I see Alex in the canoe. The shaft of his paddle knocks against the aluminum loud enough to sound like a drum. Head turned the other way, he dips the paddle into the water and steers the canoe in a lazy drift. Lying on the rise in the ground, I can see him. And that's when I know that Mom could see us. If she was still conscious when she was lying here, and if her eyes were open, she would have seen me luring Alex into the canoe. She would have heard the clang when I threw the cookie tin into the boat. She would have caught sight of Stick's small body wriggling into the canoe. Maybe she saw that I got into the canoe after him and started to paddle with my hands. Maybe she knew that we got away.

Acknowledgments

I would like to send a heartfelt thank-you to my editor, Sarah Murphy. Also to Reagan Arthur, Amanda Lang, Karen Landry, Allison Warner, Kristin Cochrane, Nita Pronovost, Nicola Makoway, Liz Foley, Michal Shavit, and Denise Bukowski for bringing this book to life. And to my family and friends Wendy Cameron, Susannah Cameron, Amy Fisher, Jim and Mary Fisher, Dany Chiasson, Sarah Wright, Olivia and Max Wright Sinclair, Jim Bull, Emily Sewell, and Erin Mulligan.

About the Author

Claire Cameron's first novel, *The Line Painter,* was nominated for an Arthur Ellis Award for best crime first novel and won the Northern Lit Award from the Ontario Library Service. Cameron's work has appeared in the *New York Times,* the *Globe and Mail,* and *The Millions.* She worked as a wilderness instructor in Ontario's Algonquin Park and for Outward Bound. She lives in Toronto with her husband and two children.

BACK BAY · READERS' PICK

Reading Group Guide

The Bear

A Novel

by Claire Cameron

An online version of this Reading Group Guide is available at littlebrown.com.

A conversation with Claire Cameron

In your introductory note, you write that The Bear *is based on a real-life bear attack that happened in 1991 with no clear reason. Tell me what about this attack struck you and compelled you to eventually write this book.*

When I first heard about the attack, I wanted to find out the reason that it happened. It was reported in the newspapers, but there was little detail about why. I worked in Algonquin Park, the wilderness area where the attack took place, the summer after. The other counselors and I would swap stories about it. I think we were all seeking consolation by trying to find out what the couple who were attacked did wrong. This is a common reaction to a tragic event. If you can isolate a reason why it happened, or a mistake that the people made, then perhaps it's only a matter of not repeating that mistake to keep yourself safe. As I came to learn more about the attack, I understood that the couple did nothing wrong. It was just a tragedy. This was the scariest conclusion of all. It stuck with me.

Did you toy with telling the story from a different point of view? Why or when did you add the children?

I didn't really think about adding the kids or anything else while doing the first draft. I had the child's voice in my head. It followed me around for some time until I realized it was developed enough that it could tell me about anything (I am a runner and have these crazy conversations with myself while pounding the streets). I had finished another book, so I thought I would just see what the voice might tell me. When I sat down to write, the idea of a bear popped to mind. By that point, the Algonquin Park attack was etched into me. I used my memories of it as a structure. All the thinking and questioning came in later drafts, when I rewrote and edited . . . then rewrote some more.

What questions did you ask of your child narrator to articulate her point of view?

Once I had the voice, it was more a matter of challenging Anna, the child narrator. I know the setting, Algonquin Park, so well that this felt quite natural. The process of writing was much closer to acting than anything I've done before. Each morning I would slip into a role and write.

When I think of it, I was in Anna's world almost entirely as I wrote the first draft. Maybe the acting part came more at the end of the day, when I had to pretend to be present for my family. I didn't tell my husband what I was working on, but after I finished the first draft I confessed that I'd been writing something intense. He laughed and said, "Yeah, no kidding." Maybe I'm not such a great actor after all.

Did you create rules or standards for developing Anna's narrative?

Not during the writing of the first draft. While I was rewriting and editing, I kept a sort of style sheet to make sure that terms and language were consistent, though I let some things vary, as I'd observed my son doing the same. My editor at Little, Brown, Sarah Murphy, was very thorough about pointing out places where I'd slipped.

The syntax of some of your sentences are so great. "I open my mouth and she turns the spoon and it goes plop and there is a little bit of Tang but then it goes wiggle wiggle and oh yuck that's weird and my tongue says no thanks and tssssuffff I spit." Are sentences like these based on real five-year-olds' dialogue?

Yes. My son was five when I started writing. We had many conversations, and I taped a few of his rants to get the rhythm. But it didn't take all that much research. He was going through a very chatty stage, so I had his speech patterns pretty much seared into my brain. As I wrote, Anna separated from him and became her own character, but quite a few of the funnier lines are directly from his mouth.

What have you learned from Anna?

I noticed that my son at age five could swing from tears of distress to belly laughs in seconds. This comes from the ability to live in the moment. It's a great coping mechanism and something that we, as adults, often struggle to do. And this is what I learned from living in Anna's world for a while. Each moment can have a value of its own.

This interview was conducted by Claire Luchette and originally appeared on Bustle.com on March 5, 2014.

Hiking alone in bear country

by Claire Cameron

I'd been hiking up, up, up for hours. I marched past the endless trees that edged the steep mountain trail. I leaned against one of those trees to rest and, exhausted, wondered if I could keep going. This particular tree was a jack pine, a scrubby-looking thing with thin bark and shallow roots. Come to think of it, I could have described myself the same way. I was twenty-one years old, fresh from a bad breakup, and hiking alone in the Canadian Rockies. It is grizzly-bear country, among many other things, but I wasn't thinking much about bears. I looked ahead and, with relief, saw what looked like a hint of high alpine meadow through the trees. A few more steps and I'd gain the wide views that I'd come to see. The mountains, heavy bodies that twist up from the glacier-scraped valleys, are topped with old peaks that jut out from ridged jaws of rock. Cold blue lakes spread out among them like fingers. I didn't know what I was looking for in the high country, but I thought that I might find something in that beauty. I pushed away thoughts of the chocolate bar that was in my pack, picked up a heavy booted foot, and quickly rounded the bend. That's when I saw it. In my path, about a hundred yards ahead, there was another body. It had brown fur with a cinnamon tinge that was draped across dense, humped back muscle. A broad head and a curved muzzle lifted to catch my scent. I knew bears. This was a grizzly. For the first time in two days, I wasn't alone.

A young woman hiking alone in the mountains sounds dangerous. In the pre–cell phone era it was, but I'll stop short of calling it foolish. By that time I was a competent rock climber and versed in mountain travel. I'd decided to strike out. Maybe I thought that the trip might prove my newfound independence, but trying to press logic on my twenty-one-year-old self is likely impossible. As I remember, the idea popped into my head. And then, just as suddenly, I hoisted on my backpack, tied a bandanna over my braid, and set off for higher altitudes.

The bear stood next to a clump of brush. Though my experience was mostly with black bears, I knew I didn't want to catch it by surprise.

"Yo, bear, yo!" I shouted the common refrain used to warn of human presence. I meant to make a booming call. It came out more like a thin yodel. I glanced around for signs of cubs. Mother bears with babies are known to be more aggressive. Fur-lined ears catching the sun, the bear slowly turned her head toward me and then looked away. My thoughts turned to my pack. It was filled with food for the remaining three days. Earlier that spring, I had my pack stolen by a black bear. He had cut a new zipper with a claw and nimbly gained access to my peanut butter sandwich. Once mugged, I'd come away from the experience feeling outwitted rather than scared. But this bear was bigger. Much bigger. If this bear wanted my sandwich, she could have it. And I'd even throw in my chocolate bar to seal the deal. My hand went to the belt of my pack at my hips. I unclipped it.

The bear must have heard the click because her head turned

to look. I was being monitored. I let the pack drop on the ground to detach myself from any source of extra interest. I kept up my weak yodeling and I took a step backward. With the bear in sight, I backed up along the path until I was at the corner. Another step, and I moved around the top switchback. I was now in the trees and standing beside the jack pine where I had rested before. The problem: I could no longer see the bear.

Realistically, the riskiest part of my trip was probably driving to the trailhead over the high mountain pass in the old van that I'd hastily bought. I called my van Lou. I'd had her brakes checked but doubted that we could stop on a dime, or even a hill. Lou had issues with radiator fluid. She didn't like it much and always wanted to leave it behind. When we finally pulled up to the trailhead of this hike, I felt relieved. As I got my pack and supplies ready for the five-day loop, I assumed that the hard part was over. Perhaps that's why I didn't even flinch when I saw the warning sign at the trailhead. There were grizzly bears active in the area.

I did think more of the sign, however, as I stood—now pack-less and unable to see the bear—leaning up against the jack pine. It had lost needles in its lower half and many of the branches had dropped, which left good places to grab hold. I barely remember climbing. Judging by the scratch marks that I later found on my arms and legs, I didn't let much get in my way. I got up as high as I could and found a branch thick enough to sit on. From there, I looked out, hoping to catch sight of the bear, but the brush obscured my view. I knew a black bear could easily scramble up after me, but the tree probably wouldn't support the weight of a grizzly. A male can weigh between four hundred and six hundred pounds, and a female half that. Either way, I knew that while my choice of tree might stop the grizzly from climbing, a creature with that much power could easily give the trunk a shake and have me on the ground in seconds. I was under no illusions. If that bear wanted to come after me, climbing a tree would only buy time.

So what did I do? I saw only one real choice. I sat in the tree and sniveled. I say "sniveled," as I was crying and scared, so it came out in a series of small, messy sobs. I also say "sniveled," as it wasn't a proud moment. As I sat in the tree, unable to see the bear, I only had time to think of my shortcomings. What was I doing? Why had I come to the Rockies alone? Why, of all the trees in the world, had I chosen an especially scratchy one with a thinner trunk to climb? Eventually, I stopped sniveling. I lost track of time.

I often think back to that stint in the tree. Now, as a novelist, my days sometimes feel like I did in that tree. I make up stories and hope that someone wants to read them. I often feel exposed and alone. Sometimes I get scared. Sometimes I invite my characters to climb up with me. When I put them in the tree, I get to watch what they do. In doing so, I get to know them completely. This is what it felt like to write my novel *The Bear*. It's about two children lost in the wilderness. The older girl takes care of her young brother. Putting her in that situation felt scary, but it also meant that I got to see how she worked. And why. It's a way to understand what's inside.

I couldn't snivel in that tree forever.

"Yo, bear," I called as I landed back on the ground with a thump. I'm not sure how long I stayed up in the tree, but it must have been over two hours. At some point, I realized I had to climb down. I crept around the corner and saw my pack lying on the trail. It was untouched. I walked to it and looked out. No bear. Where was it? I scanned up and down the meadow. No signs. I wasn't sure what to do, but there was one thing that had asserted enough of a pull to get me out of the tree. The chocolate bar. I ate it, fast. I licked the wrapper and my shaking fingertips. It tasted so good.

Then, I had a choice. Retrace my steps or keep going? I was just two days into a five-day hike. I'd finally gained the high-country views and had three days to go. There was a bear...somewhere. I knew she hadn't come back down the trail. She was probably ahead, but just as likely she may have walked away and could be somewhere down below. I wiped my nose and stopped sniveling. The bear had showed no signs of ag-gression. In fact, other than my tree climbing, nothing out of the ordinary had happened. This could be just another day, if I chose to see it that way. It's not actually safe in a tree, and run-ning back to Lou might be dangerous too. These are only ways to feel safe.

I remind myself of that as I grow older and take more risks in my writing. I need to keep wandering out alone. And that's ex-actly what I did that day. I strapped on my pack and kept hiking through the meadow. It was a magical day, and I found spectacu-lar things in the high country on that hike. Even though I knew there were bears.

Questions and topics for discussion

1. Do you think Anna's parents take too big of a risk in bringing such young children on a canoe trip? Would you take your young children camping?

2. What do you think happened between Anna's parents before the canoe trip? How clearly can Anna see their situation?

3. Is the relationship between Anna and Stick typical for children their age and gender? What kinds of conflicts does Anna have with Stick, and how does their relationship alter as the novel progresses?

4. Over the course of the book, Anna steps into the role of caring for Stick. Were you surprised by this? Do you think many young children would do this for their siblings?

5. How does Anna get back to the water's edge so that the rescuers can find her and Stick? What drives her to be able to do this?

6. How aware do you think Anna is of what happened during the bear attack and of the dangerous circumstances she and Stick face? Does her level of awareness change during the book? If so, how?

7. How does Anna cope with what happens after she and Stick are rescued?

8. Anna and Alex go back to visit the island when they are older. How is this return different for each of them?

9. What does Anna gain from going back to the island? Is this something you could have done?

10. How does Anna view the bear? Does her view change over the course of the story?

11. What did you think about reading this novel from the point of view of a five-year-old child? How would another point of view have changed things?

12. Have you ever had an encounter with a bear or other wild animal? Share your own stories of wilderness adventure and survival.